They remind us o

They are all said

They are modern

The stories you are about to read are all said to be true —
you might well have heard one or two of them yourself.
The friend who told them to you almost certainly
started by saying something like: 'This is true —
honestly! It happened to a friend of a friend of mine . . .'

These 'friend-of-a-friend' stories have become modern
myths but many of them are modern only in their detail.
Some have been around for hundreds of years and are
told in regional variations all over the world. Although
the detail may change, friend-of-a-friend stories will
not go away because they appeal to the deepest fears
and fascinations that are in each and all of us.

As long as we continue to dream, as long as we
continue to have nightmares, myths of the macabre
will continue to happen to friends of our friends.

And who knows? One day, perhaps, that friend-of-a-
friend could be you. So if you ever find yourself giving
a lift to an oddly beautiful but silent hitch-hiker or
getting strange phone calls when you're baby-sitting —
do take care. You have been warned.

Other titles to enjoy from Transworld
Publishers Ltd:

Doubleday hardback
SENSATIONAL CYBER STORIES
GRIPPING WAR STORIES
by Tony Bradman

JOHNNY AND THE BOMB
THE CARPET PEOPLE
by Terry Pratchett

Corgi paperback
AMAZING ADVENTURE STORIES
FANTASTIC SPACE STORIES
INCREDIBLY CREEPY STORIES
Edited by Tony Bradman

THE TEENAGE WORRIER'S GUIDE TO
LIFE
by Ros Asquith

THE VANISHING
HiTCH-HiKER

THE VANISHING HITCH-HIKER
A CORGI PAPERBACK ORIGINAL: 0 552 54585 6

First publication in Great Britain

PRINTING HISTORY
Corgi edition published 1998

Set in Palatino by
Phoenix Typesetting, Ilkley, West Yorkshire.

Corgi Books are published by Transworld Publishers Ltd,
61–63 Uxbridge Road, Ealing, London W5 5SA,
in Australia by Transworld Publishers (Australia) Pty. Ltd,
15–25 Helles Avenue, Moorebank, NSW 2170,
and in New Zealand by Transworld Publishers (NZ) Ltd,
3 William Pickering Drive, Albany, Auckland.

Printed and bound in Great Britain by
Cox & Wyman Ltd, Reading, Berkshire.

THE VANISHING HITCH-HIKER

Modern Myths of the Macabre

Roy Apps

Illustrated by David Wyatt

CORGI BOOKS

CONTENTS

THE VANISHING HITCH-HIKER

THE
VANISHING
HiTCH-HiKER

'Happy birthday, son!'

Rob's father steered him out through the front door to the drive. A small red Mini sat there; squat and spotless as if it had just dropped out of the sky. Rob had known for some weeks that he was going to get a car for his eighteenth birthday. All the same he couldn't help sounding surprised.

'Dad . . . ? A Mini?'

Rob was an only child. He knew how to get what he wanted. For Christmas it had been a series of driving lessons. And when he had passed his test (at the first attempt of course), just ten months after his seventeenth birthday, Rob knew that he was going to get a car for his eighteenth.

Convincing his parents had been easy really. The casual mention of a close shave (imaginary, of course) that he'd had with a maniac milk-tanker driver while out on his bike had sent his mum's face wild with worry: 'It's not safe anywhere on a bicycle these days. Really it isn't . . .'

The flowers, still regularly replaced, on the grass verge of the sharp bend where Shane Perkins had lost control of his Yamaha motorcycle told their own story. Rob never failed to mention them every time they passed the spot on their way to his grandmother's.

So for his eighteenth birthday, a car it was – but a *Mini*? Rob had spent a whole six months alerting his father to the positive benefits of Golfs and Fiestas. Rob's eye caught the letters on the number-plate and he recoiled with a look of horror.

'It's a P reg!'

And indeed it was. Though the 'P' in question wasn't at the beginning of the number-plate, denoting a 1996 or 1997 car, but at the end. Rob's new car was over twenty years old.

'There's only fifteen thousand miles on the clock,' explained Rob's dad. In truth, Rob's parents were not at all well off and the owner of the small garage in the village had by chance managed to get hold of this old, but hardly used, Mini incredibly cheaply.

Rob sighed and slid sullenly into the driver's seat. OK, so it wasn't an XR3, and it was older than he was, but it *was* a car. It would have to do. Even an old Mini would turn a few of the local girls' heads his way. In a village where the last bus from the town left at twenty past six, a car – any car – was something more than just a status symbol. And although Rob had gone on for a year now about how a car was the only thing he really wanted, that wasn't the truth. What he really wanted most of all was a girlfriend.

'I couldn't bear the thought of you out on that push bike any longer.' His mum had come out now. She pulled her dressing-gown tight about her.

'And a car's much safer than a motorbike,' his father said.

'Particularly with all the mugging going on these days,' added his mum. 'Did you hear about that poor boy who was left for dead in the gutter and the doctors found that someone had taken a knife to him and—'

'Was that the axe murderer?' asked his father.

'No! This was something else.'

Rob winced. He hated it when his parents

started on their double act like they were a kind of geriatric Sooty and Sweep.

'Yeah . . . Thanks, Mum. Thanks, Dad. It's just what I wanted.'

'Drive carefully, won't you, Robert dear . . . ?' pleaded his mother.

He did. He drove very carefully and very slowly all the way round the village green. Twice. When he finally drew up by the bus shelter, a few of the lads came over, but they were the younger ones.

'My brother's Cavalier would beat that,' said one of them

Rob ignored him.

A couple of the girls peered at the car, but they did not look at Rob. He called out of the window: 'I'm going into town tonight, if anyone wants a lift in . . . ?' Nobody answered. 'Or back . . . ?'

They ignored him. Rob thought he caught the word 'party' on their lips as they whispered amongst themselves. He pulled away and hit the hooter hard and sharp. That made them all jump and turn round. Rob grinned slyly at them as he passed. He got a few scowls and a couple of rude gestures in return.

Rob had half expected Stourford to be busy and buzzing with people. It wasn't. It was quiet; indeed, if anything, Saturday evening was even quieter than a weekday afternoon. Most of the people out seemed to be in pairs. Rob watched a couple go into a disco he had heard some of his classmates talk about. He peered round the door into the darkness within. A heavy bass throbbing shook the floor.

'What you after then, sonny?' The hard eyes of a professional doorman stared into his face. Startled, he stepped back and slunk away. It would've been different if he'd had a girl with him, he was sure.

He ended up with a cheeseburger and a root beer in McDonald's. Two girls – no more than thirteen either of them – nudged each other and giggled. He guessed they were laughing at him. He wondered who was having the party in the village and how many girls would be there.

He cruised along the riverside for a bit and was glad when the storm-laden sky darkened early. At least he had an excuse to go back home now. His parents would not find his early return surprising.

14

'Don't blame you calling it a night in weather like this, dear!'

As he took the left-hand fork away from the town centre, the first clap of thunder sounded. By the time he reached the brightly painted warehouses on the edge of town, the rain was coming down in great slants and it was as dark as a November midnight. The first storm of summer.

Bluebell Hill was on his way home. A long, steep haul up the side of the downs. As Rob began the climb he changed down a gear. The rain was so heavy now, it hit the windscreen in great bubbling waves, so that the wipers had trouble washing it away. It pounded on the roof, sounding like a million angry little fists trying to get in.

Suddenly, Rob felt very vulnerable. And scared. With a start, he realized that he had never actually driven alone before; not until this evening. He had always been with his driving instructor or his parents. Something stuck in his throat and he swallowed hard. If only there were somebody with him.

He stared ahead, fixing his eye on the furthest point of the headlight beam as it hugged the grass verge. He stared harder.

There was something . . . *someone* there! Was it . . . ? He slowed right down. The form of the figure became clearer. Yes. It was definitely a girl. Although she wasn't actually hitching, she had to be looking for a lift on a night like this.

For the briefest of moments Rob hesitated. He'd heard stories of maniac killers hitching lifts from passing motorists. But no, this was most definitely a young girl, not a thug. He drew up alongside her, leaned over and wound down the passenger-side window. Spats of rain hit his cheeks and nose.

'Can I give you a lift?'

The girl nodded quickly, opened the door and slid in. Rob leaned across her to wind up the window. She was wearing an old-fashioned long black velvety skirt which his mother no doubt would have described with a sneer as 'an Oxfam reject'.

As they drove off, Rob turned to look at her. Her clear blue eyes caught his with just the hint of a smile. He felt a flutter of excitement.

'Where are you going?'

The girl didn't seem to hear him. She was busy untying a white silky scarf, which she wore, like a cravat, around her neck. She began wrapping it lightly about her fingers.

Rob found himself having to concentrate on the road again as they neared the sharpest bend on the hill. He heard the girl utter a faint gasp. Out of the corner of his eye he saw that she was gripping the sides of her seat and shaking. Her eyes stared straight ahead. He changed down a gear.

'It's all right.' He smiled, uneasily. 'I know this road like the back of my hand.'

To his consternation, he saw her open her mouth again, this time wide as if she was going to scream, but no sound came out. Even taking the bend at a steady thirty-five, the camber still pulled the car menacingly close to the grass verge and the deep ditch beyond it.

Once the road straightened out again, even Rob sighed with relief. 'It's a bit of a nasty one, that,' he said.

The girl seemed to have relaxed too. She turned and smiled again. Rob saw a face more soft and tender than any face he had seen before. He reckoned she was sixteen, perhaps seventeen – certainly no older than he was.

His heart beat fast as they reached the brow of the hill. He ventured to turn and look at her again and was rewarded with another wistful smile. 'I'm Rob, by the way . . .'

'Carrie . . .' he heard her whisper, slowly. 'Carrie . . .'

'I'm actually going over to Boarley, but I'd be more than happy to drop you off home, if you'd like. It's a dreadful night . . .' He hoped she lived miles away; that the journey would last for ever.

Carrie pointed to the approaching road sign and drew a long finger slowly towards the left.

'Haseley?'

She nodded and looked so intently into Rob's eyes that, in his efforts to change quickly down into second, he crashed the gears. Badly.

'Sorry.'

She straightened her skirt.

Being on the other side of the hill, Haseley was not a village Rob knew at all. The unfamiliar lane narrowed alarmingly. Haseley was its sole destination. There were no villages beyond.

Large oaks and overhanging hedgerows now cut out some of the worst of the weather, but oddly for a summer storm, it seemed to have brought a chill to the air. Rob checked his window. It was done up.

'If you're cold I can put the heater on.'

She gave him that wistful smile again. Rob's left hand found the heater control. It was already on.

'That's odd. Must be something wrong with it. Known for their naff heating, old Minis. I only got the car today. Birthday present.' He was gabbling, he knew.

He turned to her, but she was looking away.

'I'm in my last term at Stourford High. I'm hoping for a job in a bank or something like that. What about you . . . ?'

Rob thought he heard her sigh, but she didn't say anything. He didn't want to press her to talk. He could sense that there was something troubling her. Well, there had to be. Why else would she have been stood there halfway up Bluebell Hill, trying to hitch a lift, alone, on a night like this? She'd probably been dumped there after a row with her boyfriend. Rob suddenly felt very protective. The lights picked out a large reflective sign saying Haseley.

'Soon be home now.'

Carrie was peering out of the side window as intently as a young child would on a train journey. They passed a dimly lit pub and a couple of cottages. Rob slowed to a crawl.

'Just say when . . .'

Suddenly Carrie jabbed a finger at the window. Rob stopped the car.

'Home?'

She nodded. A small white gate glistened in the middle of a long, high hedge. Rob peered out, but could see nothing but driving rain. As she put her hand on the door handle, it seemed to Rob as if a mighty wave of sadness suddenly overwhelmed her. Her eyes were glassy; full of tears. He felt in his pocket. He hadn't got a hankie or a tissue or anything. Carrie had already opened the door. Rob's heart thumped madly.

'Look . . . look I can see you're upset and that . . . but if you'd like to meet up some time . . . I mean . . .' He was gabbling again; he knew it.

Carrie smiled. So, so sadly this time. But her lips whispered 'Yes . . .'

Then she turned and was gone. There was no point following her to her door. Not tonight, Rob knew that. Besides, he knew where she lived. And he had the perfect excuse for calling tomorrow; her white silk scarf lay on the passenger seat beside him.

As he turned the car round and headed back towards the main road, his cheeks began to glow. Odd, but it was really quite warm in the car now. His left hand felt for the heater control. Just as he thought. It was working again.

He left it until late the following afternoon before venturing out to Haseley again. Somehow Sunday morning didn't seem a proper time to visit a girl. And Sunday lunchtime was the one time in the week when his presence at lunch was absolutely insisted on.

Carrie's scarf had a curious smell – sort of musty. Rob couldn't put a name to it, but then he was no expert on the kinds of perfumes that girls dabbed around their necks. It wasn't a plain scarf, he now noticed, but was patterned with tiny purple flecks. He had been careful to take it in and hide it in his wardrobe. It didn't seem right to leave it in the car and anyway, he wasn't keen on his mother nosing round the car and spotting it on the passenger seat. An interrogation would have been bound to follow: *'What's her name, dear? Where did you say she was from? Is she still at school or does she work? Why don't you bring her home for tea?'*

It didn't bear thinking about.

Carrie was in his head all the way to Haseley. In fact, she hadn't been out of his head since the previous evening: the wistful smile, the clear blue eyes, the way she wound her white silk scarf around her long fingers.

The afternoon sun was warm on his cheeks as he parked the car by the hedge, walked through the white gate and then stopped.

He had expected a pretty front garden. And indeed, the place he found himself in had flowers and lawns in abundance. What turned the butterflies in his stomach first to nausea and then quickly to terror was the fact that the flowers here were in vases at the foot of headstones and the lawns were closely clipped pathways between them.

Rob was standing in a graveyard. Not an ancient graveyard of anonymous weatherbeaten ragstone slabs, but a modern graveyard, half full of bright granite and marble slabs.

'Was it you who brought her back last night?'

With a start Rob spun round. A woman, pale, white-haired, oldish, but by no means elderly stood just a metre or so behind him. She held a bunch of fresh chrysanthemums in her hand. She did not seem in the least surprised to see him there.

'I'm sorry. I must have startled you. Only

I was at my cottage window and saw you walking through the gate.'

The hair on the back of Rob's neck burned furiously and when he tried to speak, he found that his mouth was as dry as a stone. He wasn't sure what unnerved him most, the start he'd had when the woman had spoken, or the familiar wistful smile she gave him with those clear blue eyes. He forced his head into a mechanical nod and then somehow found his voice.

'Carrie . . . ?'

'My daughter.'

'She was hitching a lift – just a little way up Bluebell Hill. I dropped her off at the gate . . .'

But the woman was already walking away from him. She stopped by a white memorial stone, on top of which a carved angel knelt in an attitude of prayer.

Unable to do anything else, Rob followed her. Minutes seemed to pass before he dared to look down at the inscription on the grave:

CARRIE
In Loving Memory of our darling daughter
Carolyn Anne Hunnisett
Tragically taken from us 28 May 1975
aged seventeen years

Rob was numb, but the woman beside him was quite calm as she spoke.

'That evening, she went into Stourford with her friends and had a row with a boy. So she left them and decided to hitch home – not such an unusual thing for a girl to do in those days. A lorry driver took her as far as the bypass turn off at the bottom of Bluebell Hill and then . . . well, we suppose she must've started to walk up the hill. At any rate, she was knocked down on that very sharp bend half way up.' She spoke very quietly. 'She'd been dead some hours when they found her in the ditch.'

He didn't believe her. He didn't want to believe her. She was mad. Sick. He clenched his hands together to stop himself shaking. The white silk scarf was wound so tight around his fingers that he gasped in pain. The scarf. That was *real*! 'No . . . No! I don't believe you. You're sick you are . . . !' Angrily, he waved the scarf in the woman's face; taunting her with it. 'What's this then, eh?'

She didn't flinch. 'I still keep all of Carrie's things in the attic. Sometimes at this time of the year, something goes missing. Sometimes she leaves it here for me.' She caught Rob's eye,

'But sometimes she gives it to someone to bring back.'

Carrie's old-fashioned dress; her terror as they had taken the sharp bend; her faraway look; the strange chill in the car; the musty scent of the scarf . . . still he didn't want to believe. He unwound the scarf from his fingers, feeling its soft silkiness all the time as he did so.

'Thank you . . .'

As Rob handed the woman the scarf, he saw that the purple flecks were spots of dark blood. Suddenly, he wanted deperately to be somewhere else. Anywhere else.

'I'm so sorry . . . sorry . . .' he stammered, backing away towards the gate. Though in truth, he was as sorry for himself as for the elegant white-haired woman standing before him.

He didn't have to ask her, he knew, but he found himself saying, 'Did they ever find the car . . . the one that knocked her down?'

Mrs Hunnisett shook her head. 'No. All the police were able to establish was that the car which killed Carrie must have been a popular make – that's why they never found it . . .' She paused and turned her eyes towards the lane. 'And – it was red.'

The only way he could drive home was to pretend that he wasn't really in the car. He drove recklessly and mindlessly fast. Concentrating not on the road, but on his hands and legs, just to stop them shaking.

Rob sold his red Mini within the week. His mum was hurt; his father bitter. It was the first time he'd really defied them. They couldn't understand it and Rob wasn't going to attempt to explain.

He's got a job in the building society now. He could probably afford an XR3, but he uses the bus; gets lifts instead. He hangs round with the village crowd. Sometimes he takes out one of the local girls; they rather go for his brooding intensity and his sultry good looks.

But for Rob, their smiles are never as wistful, their eyes never as clear, as those of Carrie Hunnisett: the ghost of the very first girl he ever took out.

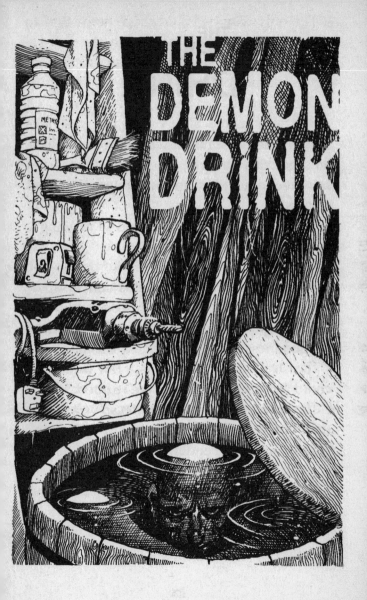

THE DEMON DRINK

Simon's dad cast him a withering look. 'Now let's get this straight. You need "just a few hundred quid like" to buy yourself a work station?'

'Yes, Dad. I've got to have one if I'm going to get this band off the ground.'

'Simon, get a life.'

Not for the first time in this conversation, Simon cringed. Where did his dad, who was old enough to have seen The Beatles in concert for goodness' sake, get such expressions?

'But Dad, if the band gets a few breaks we could be earning millions. We're good.'

'If you need this work station so very much, then you'll just have to do what I did when I wanted to buy a Fender.'

'What?'

'A Fender! Rob, Fender is to guitars what Stradivarius is to violins!'

'I know, Dad,' sighed Rob. 'I meant what did you do when you wanted a Fender?'

'I got myself a holiday job, of course. And so should you. You're old enough.'

It was easier said than done. There were no vacancies at WhoppaBurger. At the DIY super-store, they had jobs all right, but when Simon worked out the cost of his bus fares and lunch, he reckoned he would have ended up paying them for the privilege of working for them.

Then, just by chance, he got talking to Darren Trotter.

'You wanna holiday job? No probs. My dad'll take you on. Working on the buildings. Cash in hand. No questions. Know what I mean? I work for him every holiday. Get a couple of hundred a week.'

'*C'est très bon!*' said Simon. Not because he was a nerd, but because he and Darren were in French Conversation, and were therefore meant to be talking in French.

And so it was that, on the first day of the Easter holidays, Simon presented himself at Trotter's Builders' Yard. He soon found himself squeezed into the front of an old Transit van with Darren and his older brother, Jonno.

A youth by the name of Gary Mitchell, who appeared to be known affectionately as Slug, introduced himself to Simon as being 'in charge, so no effing slacking'. Slug drove the van.

Fifteen minutes later, they arrived at a large and rambling Edwardian house and garden, high up on the hill overlooking the town. Brambles and old climbing roses hung over the driveway and scratched against the roof and sides of the van. The owner stood in what was left of the front porch. A dark, dapper man of perhaps fifty, he was dressed in cords and smart brown brogues.

'Some sort of scientist geezer, name of Dr Mohammed Al-Shaq,' said Slug, as they drew up. 'Been doing research and stuff out in the Caribbean. Got a job at the University. Bought this pile.'

There was plenty to do. Rainwater pipes to be taken down, old paths to be taken up, the whole back of the house to be cleared, so that a conservatory could be built.

At dinner time, Simon, Darren, Jonno and Slug went exploring. It was Simon and Darren who found the outside steps leading down to the cellar. The door was rotten at the hinges and a shove from Darren's shoulder opened it easily. A small window, high up, afforded them just enough light to see around the white-washed walls. It was pleasantly cool. It was also empty, apart from a large wooden barrel in the far corner.

'What's that?' asked Simon. He realized that, for some reason, he was whispering.

'Soon find out,' replied Darren.

He came back with Slug and Jonno. Slug had a drill, a hammer and a small peg. 'If it stinks we can bung it up again,' he explained.

He drilled a small hole near the base of the barrel. Something begun to trickle out. Slug put his finger in and sniffed.

'Rum,' he said, getting to his feet. 'You know lads, I think this is going to be a very pleasant job. A very pleasant job indeed. Simon, old son, fetch the mugs from the van.'

They toasted themselves and their work in rum.

Simon said, 'Won't he miss it?'

'It's not exactly *his*, is it?' reasoned Slug.

Simon knitted his brows.

'I mean, he's only just moved in from abroad, hasn't he? He ain't going to have brought a frigging great barrel of rum with him, is he? Nah, this belonged to the previous owner—'

31

'Oh yeah,' Jonno said, as the penny began to drop.

'That old actress girl lived here, didn't she? She was on the telly in that comedy thing about randy doctors and nurses, years ago. They reckon she was that pickled when she died, the post-mortem doctors mistook her liver for a gherkin. This was hers all right. Poor old biddy just never got a chance to enjoy it.'

Simon's brows were still knitted.

'Come on, Si,' said Darren, 'Slug's right! Anyway, it's hardly likely to belong to the guv'nor, is it?'

'What do you mean,' said Simon.

'He's a Muslim!'

'How do you know?' asked Slug.

'You said his name was Mohammed something.'

'Eh?' said Jonno.

'Oh. Right.' Slug nodded.

'Muslims are teetotallers, aren't they?'

'Oh yeah,' said Simon, feeling slightly better about the whole idea. He was strangely uneasy about sharing a cup of rum with his workmates. He couldn't understand why: was it because it wasn't strictly theirs, or because although it was obviously rum, there was no label on the barrel telling him so?

Nevertheless, at dinner time, Simon and the others all had a little drink. Later in the week, at dinner time, they all had a larger drink. As Slug said, it helped his peanut butter sandwiches go down a real treat. Sometimes they had a drink with their elevenses, too. And with their tea break. Simon joined in with the others. How could he not? He was one of the lads, now.

The Easter holidays drifted by. Simon broke up old paving slabs, mixed cement and drank rum. He laid ballast, cleaned off old bricks and drank rum.

On the last day of the holidays, Dr Al-Shaq took Slug aside as they were all getting out of the van.

'Would you and your lads like to earn a little extra cash?' he asked.

'Doing what?' asked Slug, who although he was one never to turn down ready money, was not one to volunteer for hard work.

'I've got something I need moving up to the medical research centre at the University, where I work. It won't go in the car. And also, it's heavy.'

Simon overheard. Somehow, he knew that

what Dr Al-Shaq wanted moving was the barrel of rum.

They all stood in the cellar.

'That barrel over there? Yeah, no problem, Dr Al-Shaq,' Slug nodded, uneasily.

The doctor went off to turn his car round.

'I thought you said Muslims didn't drink.' Jonno muttered to Darren.

'I thought you said this belonged to that old actress biddy,' Darren muttered to Slug.

'Him and his mates are planning to have a right old merry time up at the University aren't they!' Slug muttered to Jonno.

'What do we do?' asked Simon, anxiously.

They all turned to Slug. He was the foreman. 'Give it a shove, lads. See how much is left inside.'

They rocked the barrel. They could hear rum slurping around inside.

'About a quarter full,' said Slug. 'So, no probs. We take the barrel out, then – oh dear, it slips from our grasp and falls on the ground. The barrel splits and the rum runs away. If we create enough panic, he won't realize that there was only a quarter of a barrel left.' He sighed. 'We lose our extra bit of cash, but that can't be helped.'

'Supposing it doesn't split,' asked Simon.

Slug took his hammer from his pouch and began pulling nails from the metal ring.

'It'll split,' he said.

Up the cellar steps they came. Huffing and puffing.

'Cor, this is a weight,' yelled Slug, pointedly. Then . . . 'Oh . . . steady with that end, Jonno . . . oh no, I can't hold it!'

The barrel fell and split. The rum flowed.

'Sorry, Dr Al-Shaq. I'm afraid you've lost your rum,' said Slug ruefully.

Dr Al-Shaq appeared resigned to the fate of his drink. 'I was going to wait until I had my colleagues with me to check the results, but still . . .'

'Results?' asked Slug.

'Yes, the results of my experiment. You see, I'm a clinical pathologist. I brought back some of my hmmmm . . . *work* from abroad using the traditional method. Just to see how well it would work. Before the days of chemicals and refrigeration and the like, bodies and limbs were always preserved in rum, you know. Now let's see . . .'

Simon wasn't listening. He was watching as Dr Al-Shaq pulled off one of the broken timbers. At first he thought he was horribly mistaken, but no; there, quite clearly, he could see a human arm.

'Excellent!' Dr Al-Shaq was saying. 'Excellent! The skin and muscle tissue is still in A1 condition! Rather ragged where it's been ripped from its late owner's shoulder blade, but otherwise still perfectly preserved! The rum has certainly done its work!'

He looked up, grinning broadly and searching the young builders' faces for a reaction. Then he quickly took a couple of steps back, acutely aware that not only did the young men all seem to be swaying somewhat and looking for something to cling onto for support; they also looked as if at any moment, they were all going to be violently sick all over his newly and expensively tarmacked drive.

THE BEASTS

BENEATH YOUR FEET

THE BEASTS BENEATH
YOUR FEET

They were playing alligator hop. You had to hop along the pavement without jumping on any of the cracks. If you did, you would be sucked down into the great crocodile swamp and be eaten alive by a ferocious croc.

'Aargh! It's got me by the ankle!' shrieked Patrick as he came down in his size-eight Cats on a crack in the pavement. He squirmed around on the ground in mock agony.

'Patrick Higgins, you're an idiot!' laughed his friend Kate.

'Aargh! It bit my leg right off!' groaned Patrick, trying not to laugh.

'I can't bear to look,' giggled Kate. She turned away. And suddenly screamed.

'It's all right,' guffawed Patrick, a laugh in his voice, 'they've only eaten the one leg.'

'No, no!' Kate insisted. 'Look, Patrick, look!'

There was an urgency in her voice which made Patrick turn round. He saw what it was that had made Kate scream. About five metres away, slumped against the base of a street light was a small animal. With great trepidation, they walked up to it.

'It's dead,' whispered Kate. 'Is it the same as the others?'

Patrick nodded slowly. 'Look at the teeth marks on its neck.' Along the animal's neck was a series of clinically clean incisions, obviously from the animal which had bitten through the fox's windpipe.

'Oh Patrick, just like the cat in your front garden . . .'

'Yes,' Patrick frowned. 'And Sam's rabbits.' He shivered at the thought of his friend's blood-stained rabbits' hutches, their doors completely gnawed through.

'Better tell your brother,' mumbled Patrick.

Kate nodded. They ran all the way to her house.

Kate's older brother David worked for the council's Environmental Services department, much to his family's horror. After gaining a doctorate in animal genetics, his parents had expected him to be offered a professorship at an American university – say, in California or Florida. Instead of which, here he was back at home in a sleepy English seaside town, working as what his father called disdainfully 'a glorified dustman'. Kate didn't know what it was *exactly* that her brother did in Environmental Services, though one of the department's responsibilities was keeping the streets free of health hazards, such as dead animals.

'David!' called Kate, as she and Patrick crashed through the front door, 'there's another dead animal!'

'A fox cub with teeth marks on its neck!' Patrick filled in the details.

Kate saw her brother tense. She was puzzled. He'd spent the last ten years of his life, ever since taking GCSE Zoology, cutting up animals. David might have been described as quiet, bookish, intense even, but squeamish he most definitely was not.

'Where?' he asked tersely.

'Up on the top road—'

'How far along?' snapped David.

'Oh, I don't know,' stuttered Kate.

'It's by a lamp-post,' Patrick added.

David raised his eyes to the heavens. 'I suppose you'll have to show me. We can't risk somebody else getting there first,' he said, grabbing the keys to his council Transit from the hall.

Kate shot Patrick a look and shrugged.

'Come on!' yelled David urgently.

They all clambered into the van and were off.

As they drew up by the street light, the dead eyes of the fox cub reflected in their headlamps.

'You didn't touch it, did you?' asked David accusingly.

'No . . . no . . . David, what is all this? First that cat in Patrick's garden—'

'Then Sam's rabbits,' Patrick put in.

'So many animals dying . . .'

Her brother did not answer her. He was already pulling on a pair of rubber gloves. He tossed another pair towards her as he slid out of the van. 'One of you is going to have to help me get it into the back.' It sounded like an order.

Patrick and Kate joined David on the pavement. He was swearing under his breath.

'Don't say a word about this to anyone, you understand?' His tone was sharp.

'David, what is going on?' Kate's voice had an edge of desperation to it.

'There's no need for you to know.'

'If you want us to help you, there is.' Kate was pouting.

David grunted and sighed. 'OK, OK, but not a word to anyone else.' He took a deep breath. 'You've already seen this corpse and a couple of others.' Roughly, he pulled the fox's head to one side. 'What do you think made those teeth marks?' Kate turned her head.

'Another fox?' suggested Patrick.

'Foxes don't usually turn on each other.'

'A dog . . . a rottweiler or something,' said Kate.

David shook his head. 'A rat,' he said, quietly.

'What, with a jaw that big?' Patrick gasped.

'Now help me get this corpse into the van,' muttered David.

As he locked the back doors of the van, David seemed to be thinking. 'I think I'd better take you two with me,' he said. 'It's obviously still about here somewhere . . .'

'What is, David?' asked Kate.

'And I guess it's best that you know the truth. That way you can be careful; vigilant.'

'David, what are you talking about?'

David ushered Kate and Patrick into the passenger seats. They drove out of town, towards the new industrial estate.

'Where are we going?' asked Kate.

'My office,' replied David.

'I thought you worked at the Town Hall,' said Patrick, 'down on the sea front?'

David shook his head. 'We have an office – unmarked, of course – at the back of the carpet warehouse.'

'Who's "we"?' asked Kate.

'Special Projects Unit.' David sighed. 'Kate, surely *you* don't believe I'm a glorified dustman, do you? Dustman, maybe, but hardly glorified. Yes, it's my job to dispose of old Freddy Fox in the back, but not before he's been through the path. lab. Not before all kinds of samples have been taken from those wounds to his neck.'

'Why?' asked Patrick.

'As you saw, it was not an ordinary rat that killed our fox.'

'You're sure it was a rat, though?' Kate asked.

David nodded. 'You've seen rabbits and a cat, we've seen many more. This is our first fox, though. All killed by our friend *rattus rattus albinus*, or the albino rat. Typically half a metre in length—'

'What!'

'Pure white and almost totally blind, but

43

with a ferocious killer instinct. Well, you saw the fox.'

'Where do they come from?' asked Kate.

'No-one's quite sure, though they may have bred from unwanted pet rats that have been flushed down the loo. Because the one thing we know for certain about *rattus rattus albinus* is that he lives in the town's sewers. That's why he is white – lack of exposure to light, and why he is almost blind, dependent entirely on a sense of smell and touch.'

Patrick shivered.

'Two other things about *rattus rattus albinus*: he's immune to all known rat poisons and he's breeding fast, as rats are inclined to do. So much so that increasing numbers are heading out of the sewer system, especially at night, in order to scavenge for food. It is only a matter of time before one of them bites a human.'

'And then . . . ?' whispered Kate. 'It'll be nasty, especially if it's a child,' said David. 'But it all really depends on what diseases it might be carrying. Now you know why Her Majesty's Government's Infectious Diseases Research Laboratory have seconded an animal pathology expert to the town council.'

'*You*, David?' whispered Kate.

'Me, sis.'

They pulled up round the back of the carpet warehouse. A security guard came out and helped David with the dead fox. They disappeared through a tall wire gate. Patrick found himself gripping Kate's hand while they waited for David to return to the van.

Nobody spoke on the way home.

When they pulled up outside Patrick's house David said, 'Not a word to anyone mind you.'

'Of course not,' said Patrick.

'Not that you'd get very far,' said David. 'I'm listed in the council's books purely as an Environmental Health Officer.'

Next day, Kate and Patrick sat on the beach, watching wave after wave pull at the shingle, bringing with it battered plastic bottles, kiddies' mangled shoes and all the other detritus of the sea. It was a warm enough day for a swim, but there were no bathers. The long brown cylinder of the sewer outlet pipe just a few hundred metres away told why.

Neither Kate nor Patrick had been able to think of anything else other than the extraordinary events of the previous night.

'You know what I think, don't you,' said Patrick, finally. 'I think your brother's a wind up merchant.'

'He's always had a macabre sense of humour,' agreed Kate, with a chuckle. 'When I was about six, he told me spiders could bury their way into your body and live there. I had nightmares for months!'

They both laughed long and loud at their gullibility.

'Let's go back to your house,' said Patrick. 'And think of a way we can pay your measly brother back.'

He turned to walk back up the beach.

But Kate hadn't heard him. She was suddenly fascinated by the water lapping over a particularly large white blob. What was it? A wad of toilet paper, a funny-shaped detergent bottle? The more she looked, the more she realized that in fact the blob wasn't made of paper or plastic. It was the wrong texture. She walked to the water's edge and watched transfixed with horror as the sea rolled back to reveal a huge rat. It was the size of a large kitten. It was pure albino and its pink eyes were blind to the world.

She turned to run, but her feet sank into the pebbles.

She fell screaming onto the beach. The rat's long nose twitched and its sharp teeth grinned menacingly as it scampered out of the water towards her bare ankles.

FINGERS

Dad dangled a glistening forkful of shepherd's pie in front of his face and asked me, 'What's he like then, this Dale?'

My little sister pitched in before I'd even had time to draw breath. 'He's got acne. Urgh!'

I shoved her chair sharply with my foot and she tumbled onto the floor, squealing like a drowned rat.

Dad hoisted the *Daily Mirror* up over his head and left Mum to play the part of UN peacekeeper. She escorted my sister to a buffer zone in the front room and told me I'd be making an appearance at a war crimes trial later.

I suppose *you* want to know what Dale's like? Well, he's tall, almost six foot. He's got short black curly hair, brown eyes and he wears Cats. He likes pizza and Man United. He's seventeen and he's got a car.

'He's got a car,' I said to Dad. 'It's a Sierra.'

'Oh . . . ?' He looked worried.

'I mean he won't be leaving me standing at a bus stop waiting for the last bus home.'

'I should hope not. He'd soon get a piece of my mind if he did,' muttered Dad.

Mum came through. Dad looked at her.

'He's got a car,' he said.

'Oh, that's nice,' said Mum. 'Justine, sit down and listen to me.'

The war crimes trial had begun.

'Don't ever, ever, do that to your sister again, do you hear me?'

I sighed, then nodded.

'I've a good mind not to let you go out tonight—'

'Mum!'

She did though.

I overheard them arguing about it in the kitchen.

'He's got a car, you know,' said Dad.

'So, I'd rather have her being driven home in a car then hanging about the streets at night at her age,' replied Mum. 'You're safe in a car.'

At *her* age!

'It's a Sierra,' muttered Dad.

'So?' Mum wasn't getting the drift.

'They're big cars, with a big back seat. Do

you know what they call lads who buy Sierras?'

'No and I don't want to, thank you very much,' snapped Mum. 'Justine's a sensible girl.'

'She's fifteen,' answered Dad, 'nobody's sensible when they're fifteen.'

Thanks, Dad.

There was a hoot from a two-tone horn outside and with a quick 'bye-ee!' I was up and out of the front door, before Mum could change her mind.

I got in and Dale revved up the engine. I saw the upstairs curtain twitch and my little sister's face lurking behind it. I stuck my tongue out at her.

Dale sat there staring out of the windscreen. 'Where do you want to go?'

I shrugged.

We went to Burger King. He had a burger; I just had a shake. We talked. His favourite programme was *Baywatch*, he said. He grinned. He's got a really cheeky grin. Of course, I knew that. I'd known Dale for ages. He was in the Juniors when I was in the Infants. But I'd never really talked to him, not until the Sixth Form disco last Saturday.

'Hullo,' he'd said.

'Hullo,' I'd replied.

'You was in the Infants with our Deanie.'

'Yeah,' I'd said.

We did some dancing.

'I got a car,' he'd said. After the disco, he'd taken me home.

'Want to come out with me?'

'All right.' That had been last Saturday.

No-one else in our class was going out with a boy with a car.

Dale finished his burger. 'Where do you want to go now?' he said. That ever so cheeky smile again.

So I said, 'Dunno, somewhere in the country.'

Dale grinned again. We headed out towards the bypass, but there was a hold-up. Dale swore. 'It's the nee-nah boys!'

I could just see a couple of police officers way ahead of us. They were waving down every car.

'They must be doing some sort of check,' said Dale. 'That's all we need!'

'You are insured, aren't you, Dale?'

'Of course I am,' he snapped back. 'I just don't like the nee-nah boys, OK?'

He turned the car round and we headed back towards the town.

'We'll take this back road,' said Dale.

'Do you know where it goes?'

'Nope.' Liar. The road sign was big enough. That was how we ended up in Lovers' Wood.

It's right on top of the downs. You go along this rough, muddy track where the trees and bushes are all overgrown. Then the track gets narrower and muddier and the bushes and trees get thicker and more dense.

Dale reversed the car up the track. Twigs and leaves scraped the side. He kept revving up, then braking, making it skid. Mud splashed up all the way over the roof. I ducked. Stupid. Dale laughed.

We got out . . . It was so quiet. There weren't even any birds singing. It was quite dark too, even though shafts of sunlight would all of a sudden pierce the branches.

'It's like being in church,' I whispered.

Dale took his hand out of mine. 'Didn't know you went to church,' he muttered.

'I don't,' I said. 'I used to go to Sunday School though.'

You could hear every one of our footfalls.

The flickers of sunlight began to grow more grey. I shivered.

'Let's go back to the car, Dale.'

He put his arm round me and led me back up the track to the car.

I sat in the passenger seat. There was mud on my shoes. I kicked them off.

'You all right?' asked Dale.

'Yeah . . . it's just . . . it's so quiet.'

Dale switched on the car radio. We settled down to the music.

Then came the news. It puts you off a bit. I mean the stuff about wars and MPs you can ignore, but when they get to bits about the woman in Bognor Regis who's expecting sextuplets and the man in Bournemouth who's had his ear bitten off by his pet parrot, you have to listen, don't you? Well, I do. But Dale still had his arm round me and was nuzzling my ear.

Then the local news came on. There was only one story. A psychopath had escaped from police custody earlier in the day, while awaiting trial for the horrific murder of a young girl on her way home from an eighteenth birthday party.

'Wallies,' I said. 'The police can't do anything right.'

They had set up road blocks all over the county.

'Must've been what they were doing out by the bypass earlier,' I said.

They were interviewing the girl's mother. The girl who had been killed. I leaned right over and turned the radio off. Dale leaned right over and kissed me. He combed his fingers through my hair. I touched his face. It was all rough and prickly when I ran my fingers up his cheek and all smooth when I ran my fingers down. Dale kissed me again.

Then, all of a sudden, there was a waft of cool evening air on the back of my head. I opened my eyes and turned round. And that was when I saw the car door was open on my side. Not just open, but opening wider all the time.

It all happened in a blur.

I was screaming. 'Dale, Dale!' I pushed him off me and he fell back on the hand brake with a howl. I pulled at the door, trying to get it shut. By now I could see an outline of a startled face at the window. So could Dale. I pulled the door again. Dale grabbed the handle with me and pulled too. My hands were slippery with sweat. Slowly, the door was easing open. With a final effort, I pushed hard down with my foot against the wheel arch and Dale and I pulled hard together. The door slammed shut with a thud and I rammed my fist hard down on the lock. There was a dreadful yell from the face and a thumping on the outside of the door.

'Go!' I shouted as Dale struggled to start the engine.

The face was close up now. I could see his eyes – dark, wide and mad, the right one on me, the left one on Dale. The left one – it was lazy, or dead, or glass.

The car lurched, skidded and moved off. The face screeched some more, its right eye manic, its left eye lifeless.

'He's running alongside with us!' I screamed.

The car skidded and swayed and Dale battled to get out of Lovers' Wood as fast he could. All the time I was terrified we would get stuck in the mud, or Dale would lose control and we'd hit a tree.

Just before the road, the face appeared again, screaming 'Stop! Stop!' Then with a final hideous shriek, it seemed to give up. By the time we swung out onto the road, anyway, he'd gone.

I was shaking and sobbing. Dale was

shaking, too. We didn't say anything. Dale was concentrating on driving. The beam from the headlights bounced off hedgerow after hedgerow as the car twisted around the narrow bends.

We shot out onto the main road and Dale had to brake like mad to avoid the car coming in the opposite direction. It was a police car. It screeched to a halt, spun round and followed us, its blue light flashing. Dale was in no mood for a chase.

He stopped and wound down his window. Slowly. He was thinking what I was thinking. Yes. Slowly. Just in case . . .

The officer had silver hair. Another officer, not much older than Dale, joined him. 'That was a bit of a silly thing to do,' the older one shouted to Dale above the hiss and crackle of their two-way radios. 'You're asking to get yourself – and your young lady friend – killed.'

I started sobbing.

The police officer bridled. 'Has this young man been making a nuisance of himself, miss?'

'No!' I shook my head. 'Someone tried to get into the car!'

'Where?'

'Through the door—'

'No, I mean where were you when—'

'Oh. Lovers' Wood.'

I swear the police officer raised an eyebrow. Anyway, I know I blushed.

His younger colleague started hopping around like a cat with fleas. 'Echo Foxtrot Golf,' he yelled into his two-way radio. 'We have a possible sighting!'

'What was this man like?' asked the older officer.

I told them: the truly awful face; the screaming; the mad staring right eye; the lifeless left one.

'We have a *definite* sighting! Lovers' Wood! I repeat, Lovers' Wood!'

'The man you saw was James Arthur Tucker. He escaped from police custody earlier today. He's awaiting trial for the murder of a schoolgirl.'

I sniffed. 'I heard . . . on the radio.'

'Then you don't need me to tell you just how close you've been to an untimely end tonight.' He turned to Dale. 'Both of you. Now if I were you, I'd get this young lady home, straight away, sir.'

Dale nodded.

'You *are* all right, miss? You must've had

a nasty shock,' enquired the police officer.

'I'm fine,' I replied.

'We can provide a police escort, if you wish.'

I shook my head.

The police car roared off.

Dale started the engine. He looked at me and I saw the slightest hint of his cheeky grin return to his face. I took his hand and wound my fingers through his. He squeezed.

'Come on,' he said. 'Better get you home, like the policeman said.'

He drew up quietly outside the house. No curtains twitched. He bent over and kissed me.

'Want to come out with me again?'

'All right. Make it Ten Pin Bowling or something though.'

'Yeah,' Dale nodded. 'No more nasties.'

'No more nasties.'

I opened my door.

It seemed to jam just a little. Then I heard a gentle kind of plop! like a lump of mince dropping into a saucepan.

Instinctively, I looked down.

I heard my screams fill the night sky and echo round the houses.

There, lying on the ground under the bloodied car door that had cut them off, were three severed fingers, the letters L O V roughly, but clearly, tattooed across the bloodied knuckles.

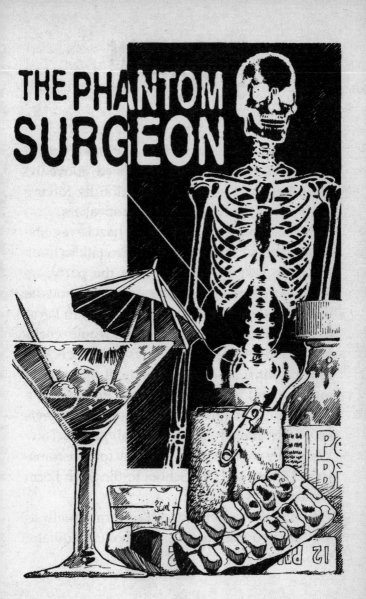

THE PHANTOM SURGEON

THE PHANTOM SURGEON

The girl was moving her lips. She was trying to make herself heard, Kieran realized, above the pounding roar of the music painfully forcing itself out of the two-metre-high speakers.

She had long black hair, dark hazel eyes. She was beautiful. And she wanted to talk to him!

Kieran cast a hazy eye over the party; he wanted the rest of his tutor group to know he was with this girl. He'd been at the Sixth Form College for two weeks now. Two whole weeks since he'd left the dreary Boys' High School – much against his mother's better judgement, it must be said. And he *still* hadn't got himself a girlfriend. But now . . . at Toby Walmsley's seventeenth birthday party of all places! Toby Walmsley was the only other boy to have transferred from the High School to the Sixth Form College with Kieran.

Suddenly, he felt the girl's warm breath as she shouted into his ear. 'The hall! It's quieter there!'

It was: not a lot, but enough to make yourself understood in conversation. She gave a quick flash of her dark eyes. 'I'm Tamsin.'

Beautiful.

'Hi, Tamsin. I'm Kieran.'

It was dark in the hall. Nobody took much notice of them. Nobody saw them leave.

She worked, she said, in one of those flash stone and glass offices in the renovated warehouses down by the river. She'd been to a private school. All girls. He could believe that. She was just eighteen. She had her own studio flat. Which was where Kieran was sitting now. In a big floppy armchair. It must be somewhere on one of the new estates, he imagined. He couldn't quite remember the route the cab driver had taken from Toby's house.

'Where do you live?' She'd smiled at him, perched above him on one of the chair's arms.

'Albion Hill.'

'That's miles away.'

'You'll never get back there tonight.'

'No.'

'You can stay here . . .'

'Yeah. Ta.'

Which was why he had her mobile phone

to his ear, listening to it ringing.

'Hello . . . ?' The voice was clear, precise, with just a tinge of anxiety.

'Mum?'

'Kieran? Are you all right?'

'Yeah . . . yeah. I'm staying at Toby's.'

'That's all right, dear. I'll see you in the morning.'

Tamsin was mixing a couple of drinks. Cocktails by the look of it. She smiled and sauntered her way across the room towards him. She seemed to be swaying.

She put the drinks down on a small table. He noticed her perfume.

She sat down on his lap. Then she put her long hand out and began to slowly stroke his neck.

Kieran was aware of a pain in his stomach. Then a pain in his head. In fact, his whole body ached. He shivered. He was cold. And wet. He put out his hand and felt the rough, curved edge of a kerbstone. He was in a dream. No he wasn't, he was in a nightmare. He opened his eyes and the throbbing in his head became a scream. He closed them again, desperate to wake himself from out of the nightmare.

He had to get out of it. He'd walk out of it into another dream, or better still, into wakefulness, into morning. He opened his eyes again. Only then did he realize the most terrible thing of all: the pavement he was lying on was a real pavement; the cold was the freshness of an early autumn morning; the pain was real pain. This was no nightmare. He was awake. This was his morning.

Each footstep made him gasp and the early morning sunlight at the end of the alleyway seemed to get no closer. Then all of a sudden, he felt its surprising warmth as it cast a long, dusty shaft up the side of the tall buildings. He reached the main road and slithered back down onto the pavement.

It was quiet. The traffic lights changed from red, to amber, to green and then all the way back again, just to amuse themselves it seemed. He heard the faint chug of a diesel engine, looked up, and saw a black cab at the lights.

The cabbie tut-tutted and shook his head. 'Blimey, you look as if you've had a right skinful, sonny Jim!' At any other time, Kieran would've hated being patronized by being called 'sonny Jim', but now, he loved it.

The cabbie hauled him into the back. 'You

throw up in my cab and I'll kick you straight out, son!' he threatened. Then he took a swift look at the state of Kieran's clothes, sniffed, turned up his nose and made him sit on the floor.

He had the sense not to let himself in at a quarter to six in the morning. He'd have questions to answer from his mother, he knew.

The postman found him on the front lawn; recognized him and rang the bell.

His mother had the decency to let him get to bed and to try and sleep it off. He didn't even bother to get undressed, but climbed straight into bed in his clothes.

But he didn't feel any better when a few hours later she began challenging him about what had happened at the party.

'How much did you drink, Kieran?'

No answer.

'It wasn't drugs, was it?'

'No, Mum!'

'It must've been something. I've a good mind to go round and see Toby's mother. Give her a piece of my mind.'

'No, Mum!'

'I don't know what she could've been thinking of, letting you get in such a state. And what were doing sleeping it off on our front lawn at *that* time of the morning?'

Kieran groaned.

'I can't imagine what the postman must have thought!' Her tongue clicked against the back of her teeth: a habit that had always infuriated Kieran. 'Can't you remember anything?'

Kieran groaned again. 'No, Mum.'

Of course he could. He could remember the dark hazel eyes, the long black hair. He could remember her long sleek finger on his neck. He could remember that her name was Tamsin.

'You must be able to remember *something*!'

He shook his head. With a loud sigh of disapproval, his mother left the room. Perhaps he should've taken more care about just what he was drinking. He remembered someone at college telling him about their cousin who had got a job on a building site and had ended up drinking . . . no, it didn't bear thinking about.

He slept – or rather dozed fitfully – the rest of the day and the night. The pain – a constant throbbing pain in his stomach – just wouldn't go away. At tea time, he was still in pain, still feverish, still without an appetite. His mother called the doctor.

'Just look straight at the torch, Kieran.' The doctor's command was flat, without emotion.

'I thought it must be drugs, doctor. You read so much about that E or whatever they call it,' Kieran's mother prattled away nervously.

'Hmm-hmm.' Still the doctor's tone betrayed nothing.

'Slip off your shirt, Kieran.'

Kieran hauled himself up onto his arms and did so, instinctively pulling up his trousers a few centimetres at the same time.

'And your vest.'

The doctor helped Kieran off with his vest.

Kieran's mother gasped.

'What is this, Kieran?' The doctor's voice was still flat and unemotional.

'Kieran! What happened?' His mother's voice was shrill and frantic.

Kieran struggled to sit up to see what all the fuss was about. Right round his midriff, just under his rib cage, was wound a thick, broad crêpe bandage. Underneath the bandage on the left side was a long bulge.

The doctor was already untying the bandage carefully, purposefully, like a knitter with a skein of wool. The bulge was revealed to be a gauze dressing. Under the dressing was a scar.

'Have you been in a fight, Kieran?'

'Kieran doesn't fight, doctor!' blubbered Kieran's mother.

The doctor ignored her. 'It would help us to help you get better if you could tell us what you remember, Kieran.'

He could remember the dark hazel eyes, the long black hair. He could remember her long sleek finger on his neck. He could remember that her name was Tamsin.

'I don't know ... I don't understand ...' he mumbled. He was close to tears.

'It's a particularly clean wound; not at all ragged. Made with a very sharp, small blade.'

But Kieran's mother wouldn't look.

'And somebody has taken the trouble to clean it and dress it quite expertly. Have you been treated at the hospital, Kieran?'

Kieran shook his head. 'I don't remember ...' he moaned.

The doctor and Kieran's mother dressed the wound. Then they dressed Kieran and took him to the hospital.

He lay waiting on a hospital trolley in a little side room in the Accident and Emergency Department.

A young doctor, not much older than

71

Kieran, examined him first. He could see the hair on her top lip as she bent down over him.

'My, Kieran, you *have* been in the wars,' she said, smiling. Her dark hair was dyed blond and she had blue eyes.

A tall, well-spoken doctor visited him next. He smelt of tobacco. 'I am Dr Raj and I am the surgical registrar,' he announced. 'It will be necessary for you to produce a urine and a stool sample.'

He was sent for X-ray. A group of medical students, all in white coats and carrying clip boards, came in, looked quizzically at him, wrote notes, said nothing and went out again.

At about tea time, a distinguished-looking gentleman sporting a pink shirt and a red bow-tie arrived. He perched on the end of Kieran's bed and peered at him over his half-moon glasses. A name-badge read: 'Mr J.P.P. Smith-Robinson. Consultant Surgeon.'

'Well, young man,' he said.

He pulled down the sheet and studied Kieran's scar. He took a small knife from a cupboard and held it up for Kieran to see. 'Well, young man,' he said again and pulled the sheet back over Kieran's stomach. 'Your wound was made with one of these.' He paused. 'A surgical scalpel.'

Kieran swallowed.

'Can you remember anything about Saturday night at all, Kieran?'

He could remember the dark hazel eyes, the long black hair. He could remember her long sleek finger on his neck. He could remember that her name was Tamsin.

Kieran shook his head. 'I had a few drinks at Toby's party and then . . .' He shrugged, and frowned in a pretence at struggling to recall even the barest of details.

'You were also drugged, a real knock-out mixture . . . assuming, as you insist, that you didn't imbibe them of your own accord.'

Kieran shook his head.

The consultant snapped up an X-ray film on a viewer on the wall.

'You were robbed, you know.'

'Was I?'

The consultant nodded.

'What did they take?'

The consultant jabbed a smart fountain pen at Kieran's X-ray film. 'Your left kidney,' he said. 'They command quite a decent price on the black market.'

*   *   *

They kept Kieran in for a couple of nights for proper post-operative observation. Then he was sent home to convalesce. The police came and asked questions, but Kieran told them nothing.

Toby remembered seeing Kieran with, 'Some bird with long hair, don't remember anything else about her, I thought she was with the Tech crowd.' And, of course, nobody had seen Kieran and Tamsin leaving the party.

A few weeks later, Kieran took a bus out to one of the outlying new estates, where he guessed her flat must have been, but he didn't find anything there to jog his memory as to its exact location.

Sometimes he would wander past the flash stone and glass offices down by the river. He never saw her.

'You mean you were that smashed, you can't remember anything?' Toby would sometimes enquire, incredulously.

He could remember the dark hazel eyes, the long black hair. He could remember her long sleek finger on his neck. He could remember that her name was Tamsin.

THE VERY LAST BABY-SiTTER

THE VERY LAST BABY-SITTER

'There's pizza in the fridge if you get hungry, Donna,' Michael's mother said.

'Thank you, Mrs Parrinder.' The very last baby-sitter smiled dutifully.

'And there's milk or cola—'

'If you get thirsty,' Michael interrupted sarcastically. He was leaning against the kitchen door.

Mrs Parrinder smiled apologetically. 'This is Michael,' she said.

'Hello, Michael,' said Donna, brightly.

'Say hello to Donna, Michael,' said Mrs Parrinder.

'Hello-to-Donna-Michael,' Michael sneered. He blew some gum in Donna's face.

'He's twelve,' said Mrs Parrinder, as if that explained everything.

'And a half,' growled Michael.

'Too young, of course, to baby-sit the twins,' Mrs Parrinder continued. 'They're upstairs asleep. Would you like to see them?'

'I'd love to,' said Donna.

Michael belched; then followed his mother and his new baby-sitter upstairs.

Their feet sank into the deep plush carpet pile as they padded along the upstairs landing.

A tall man with well-manicured hands and smelling of perfume burst out of the master bedroom. He was fumbling with a pair of gold cuff-links.

'This is my husband,' Mrs Parrinder said to Donna.

He shook Donna's hand absent-mindedly. Then he turned to his wife. 'Five minutes,' he hissed.

Mrs Parrinder edged open the nursery door. Two pink cots with white lace canopies. Two bow-tied teddy bears. Two sleeping babies, hands in their mouths, curled up, facing each other.

'Abigail,' said Mrs Parrinder softly, 'and Emily.'

'They're lovely,' gushed Donna.

Outside on the landing she heard Michael making puking noises.

'My two precious jewels,' whispered their mother. She leaned over Abigail's cot and kissed her lightly on the cheek, then she did the same to Emily.

Back downstairs Mrs Parrinder fussed over her face in the hall mirror.

Mr Parrinder bounded down the stairs and helped his wife on with her fur coat.

'We'll be back by midnight,' Mrs Parrinder said to Donna.

Mr Parrinder wagged a finger at Michael. 'You're to be in bed before half past nine, do you understand?'

Michael shrugged, sulkily.

Mr Parrinder held the front door open for his wife. A chill autumn wind blew through the house. He hurried his wife out of the front door and slammed it behind them.

The house felt very quiet. It was that sort of house. Double-glazing shut out all sounds from the outside. Thick wall-to-wall carpets shut out all noise from the inside.

Michael crept up close behind Donna. 'Aren't you going to put the chain on, then?'

Donna jumped.

'Some do; some don't,' Michael said.

Donna looked at him, quizzically.

'Some baby-sitters put it on, some don't,' he added by way of explanation. 'Mind you, I'd

78

put it on, if I was you. I mean, you never know who's out there, do you?'

'No,' said Donna, trying to make light of it and failing abysmally, 'you most certainly don't.'

'Damien Jenkins at school; a friend of his brother's girlfriend had her car broken into by a guy with a machete.'

Donna slipped the security chain on the front door.

'The only trouble,' Michael's face spread into a malevolent grin, 'is that it makes it ever so difficult to *escape*, doesn't it?'

Donna made a pretence of ignoring him and went through to the lounge. She wasn't particularly fazed by this obnoxious boy. She was sixteen, after all. She'd done baby-sitting for two whole years. She'd helped at Cub Scout camp. Not least, she had two younger brothers at home. No, silly boys didn't bother her.

'Where did they find you?' Michael asked suddenly. 'Yellow Pages?'

'They didn't find me, I found *you*,' replied Donna with a smile. She was sharp, when she needed to be, was Donna.

'Oh, the advert in Patel's window . . . or the post office?' retorted Michael, airily.

'Patel's.'

'You know, they've got adverts in the Co-op, the Service Station and the off licence. The frigging off licence! I mean, who do they really want as baby-sitters for us, druggies and winos? Help yourself to booze by the way.'

'No thanks.'

'I do,' Michael told her pointedly.

Donna didn't bat an eyelid. 'Not while I'm looking after you, you don't.'

'You know you're our fifth baby-sitter this month?'

'That doesn't surprise me.'

'There was Sally and Yolande and Birgitte – she was German . . . What do you mean, it doesn't surprise you?'

'I imagine they began to find it all a bit wearing.' Yes, she could give as good as she got, could Donna.

'What, me, do you mean?' asked Michael, innocently.

'Well, I wasn't exactly thinking of your little sisters.'

Michael looked steadily at Donna. 'Half sisters.'

'Half sisters, sorry.' Donna couldn't avoid the edginess in her voice. A bit of a blush came to her cheeks. She had been wrong-footed.

'*He*'s not my dad,' muttered Michael, gruffly.

'No.' Donna was still edgy.

'For your information, my surname's still Davies. Same as my mother's was before she married *him*,' Michael informed her. 'I want to watch *Dark Skies*. We've got it on video.'

'Will you go to bed when I ask you to?'

Donna saw a trace of a smirk cross Michael's lips. 'Yep,' he said.

'OK. We'll watch *Dark Skies*.'

Michael put the video on. He moved Donna's book off the sofa and sat down next to her.

'Oh, it's *this* one,' said Donna, when the opening scene came up.

'Have you seen it before?' asked Michael.

Donna nodded. 'With my brothers. Many times.' She was back to her natural, relaxed self now.

'So have I,' said Michael, not to be outdone.

They watched *Dark Skies*. In silence. No-one talks to each other when they're watching *Dark Skies*.

When it had finished, Donna said, 'Michael, it's half past nine.'

Without a word of protest, Michael got up and went to the door. 'Coming up to kiss me good night?'

'I don't think so,' said Donna.

'Why not?'

'Because you wouldn't really want me to, would you now?' replied Donna with a twinkle in her eye. 'So I'll say it now. Good night, Michael.'

'Night, Donna,' said Michael, sounding like somebody out of *The Waltons*.

Michael shut the lounge door behind him. Donna got up and opened it. She heard him pulling the chain in the toilet and going into his room. She curled her feet up on the sofa and opened *Jane Eyre*. She was doing it for GCSE. She smiled to herself. She felt she was getting the measure of Michael. She was also mightily pleased he had gone to bed with so little bother.

The twins slept quietly. Occasionally, Donna could hear tiny rustles like those of fidgety mice, coming over the baby alarm, as one or other of them turned over in her sleep.

The phone rang at five to ten. It rang for some time. No-one had bothered to tell Donna where it was. She scurried about the lounge, afraid its insistent ringing would wake the twins. She found it on the drinks cabinet, disguised as a model vintage Rolls Royce Silver Ghost. One of Mr Parrinder's big boy's toys.

'Hello . . . ?' There was a pause. 'Uhh . . . Five O double seven double four.'

Another pause.

'Hello?'

A click. Then nothing. Donna replaced the handset on the Rolls Royce. Wrong number, she thought. They were always getting them at home. She was a sensible girl, was Donna. She curled herself up again with her *Jane Eyre*.

The phone rang again at five minutes past ten.

'Hello? Five O double seven double four . . . ?'

This time Donna heard the breathing: faint, but distinct.

'Hello? Who's there?'

All she heard was a click.

Donna put the phone down on the model vintage Rolls Royce. She went back to her book. But she found it really hard to get back into the story.

The phone rang again at ten minutes past ten.

'Hello? Five O double seven double four . . . ?'

The breathing was heavier, more rhythmic.

'Hello?' Donna found her voice was sounding nervous, high-pitched.

Another click.

Donna curled up again with her book. The words seemed to bounce around in front of her eyes. She realized they didn't mean anything. She went back to the model Rolls Royce and took the phone off the hook. But she couldn't concentrate.

'Please replace the handset and try again. Please replace the handset and try again. Please replace the hand—'

Donna replaced the handset, unable to take any more of the monotonous, snooty voice. She curled up on the sofa and tried to read. But *Jane Eyre* was like pages and pages of gibberish.

And the phone was ringing again.

'Hello! Who is this?'

The breathing – heavy. Then all of sudden, a deep, crazy laugh. Donna couldn't help but give a small scream. She put the handset back. She sat down. She got up. She sat down. Then she got up again and went across to the phone and grabbed the handset, quickly, clumsily, before it could ring again. Now *her* breathing was rhythmic and heavy. She'd got to ring someone, she knew that – but who? Mr and Mrs Parrinder? They were busy watching a play about a madman who murdered his wife (*Othello* by William Shakespeare at the Theatre Royal). The police? And what could they do? Come round and offer to make her a cup of tea? No, Donna reckoned, the caller was *out there* somewhere and he had to be found.

Donna dialled. The voice, as ever, was false, mechanical. 'You were called today at twenty-two fifteen hours. The caller withheld their number.'

Donna dialled again. 'Thank you for calling B.T. Your call is being held in a queue at present. Please hold while we try to connect you.' A few tinny bars of Ravel's *Bolero* followed. 'Thank you for calling B.T. Your call is being—' A click. Then another voice. A real voice. 'Hello, BT. Trudi speaking. How can I help yee-oo?'

'Someone keeps ringing up,' blurted out Donna. 'Heavy breathing, laughing.'

'A nuisance call, do you mean, caller?'

'Yes!' Donna almost sounded frantic. 'It's horrible!'

'I see.'

'I'm on my own. Babysitting. I dialled call back, but he's withholding his number.'

'What is your number, caller?'

'Five O double seven double four.'

'Try to keep calm. I will put out a call trace and ring you back.'

'Thank you. Thank you . . .' Donna sounded breathless. The seconds ticked away.

The phone rang. Four rings . . . five rings. Donna was panicking. Was it BT – or was it the nuisance caller? Donna lifted the receiver.

'Hello, caller?'

Relief.

'Hello?'

'You rang about the nuisance calls?'

'Yes . . .'

'The call trace was positive. We have an identifiable caller. The police are on their way to the address to which the caller's number is allocated.'

'Good. Thank you.'

'Would you like a visit from a woman police officer or a specially trained volunteer visitor from the local Victim Support Scheme?'

'No. No . . .'

Sensible girl Donna. Able to take care of

herself, thank you very much. Then – 'Actually yes!' she blurted out. 'Could you ask a woman police officer to call?'

'Yes, of course. What's the address?'

'High Beeches, Links Avenue—'

Trudi couldn't conceal her shock. 'Caller? Caller? Don't move. The address of the identifiable caller? It's the same. Name of Mr M R D Parrinder?'

'Yes!'

'Are there two lines in the house?'

'There . . . must be. He has an office upstairs. Oh no. Oh no . . . ! There's a child asleep upstairs! And two babies . . . ! No!'

She didn't know how long she stood there unable to move, the phone still in her hand.

A noise behind her startled her. She turned round and saw Michael in the doorway.

'Michael!' Her voice was full of relief, but she realized she was shaking like a leaf.

'Hello, Donna!' said Michael. 'Spot of bother?' His voice was breezy – somehow unnaturally breezy.

'Are you all right? Are the twins all right?' stuttered Donna.

'I'm afraid I made a bit of a mess of their duvet covers,' said Michael, flatly.

It was only then that she saw the blood-stained knife in Michael's hand.

She didn't know how long they just stood there, facing each other. Keep calm, Donna, she was saying to herself. Just keep calm and don't excite him. 'Michael,' she said gently and slowly. 'Put that knife down.'

Michael didn't put the knife down. He held it up. It glistened in the light from the chandelier. Donna screamed as she saw the thick red blobs dripping onto the carpet.

Michael took a few steps towards her. 'I had to do it, Donna. It was the only way. Every night it's the same. They go out for meals, his business dinners, to the theatre. I'm too old for baby-sitters. In fact, Donna, you are the last. The very last baby-sitter.'

By now, blue lights were flashing across the curtains like so many strobes. They listened as the police smashed the lock on the front door.

'The chain will hold them up. I wonder whose idea it was to put that on,' whispered Michael. He waved the knife about, a few centimetres from Donna's face.

More police officers were thumping the lounge window. 'Do you remember, Donna? I told you that double-glazing takes some breaking,' hissed Michael, flashing the knife again.

Donna screamed.

There was a crash as the chain finally came away from the door.

Michael dropped the knife and put his hands in the air as the officers charged in.

Mr and Mrs Parrinder followed. The police had caught up with them in the bar during the interval.

Mrs Parrinder started screaming hysterically. Mr Parrinder went charging upstairs.

'No, sir!' yelled one of the police officers. 'Don't go up there!'

But gone up there he had.

He let out a huge cry; half laughter; half tears. 'They're all right!' he sobbed. 'They're all right!'

The officer who had taken the knife off the carpet suddenly said, 'Hey . . . this isn't blood. It's ketchup!'

'Only a few years in the police force and you can already tell the difference between human blood and tomato ketchup? Wow!' Michael said, with his customary sarcasm.

'That's enough from you,' said the police officer in charge.

'OK. It's a fair cop,' said Michael grandly. 'I'll come quietly, officer.'

'This isn't a laughing matter, sonny,' he replied, twisting Michael's arm slightly harder than necessary.

Michael couldn't say goodbye to his mother. Mrs Parrinder was still sobbing uncontrollably on the stairs. He couldn't say goodbye to his stepfather, either. Mr Parrinder was still upstairs with his daughters. So he said goodbye to his very last baby-sitter.

'All the best, Donna! There's pizza in the fridge if you get hungry. And milk or cola if you get thirsty.'

Michael did think of blowing her a kiss. But he couldn't. They'd already put the handcuffs on.

PASSPORT

LOVE.
BiTES

Souvenir From
BRAZILIA

LOVE.BiTES

I've never been out with anybody else. Not after Helena.

I'd known Helena for years. She was in the same class as me all the way through school right from Year Seven. We didn't start going out together until Year Eleven though. We were in practically all the same GCSE groups. We were both in the Drama Club and when I found myself playing Jack in *The Importance of Being Earnest* opposite Helena's Gwendolen, well, it just seemed perfectly natural.

That was the thing about Helena, she was so easygoing. I mean, with both of the other 'items' in our year, there was all sorts of anguish and angst. With Helena, it was impossible for things to be difficult. That was why we went out together for such a long time. That was why it lasted, I think.

In fact, the only bother with this was that I was always getting guys coming up to me for advice about *their* girlfriends: 'Why won't she snog me? Is she just going out with me because I've got an IQ of 250 or does she actually fancy me? Why is she so jealous of me going out with my mates for seventeen pints of lager after rugby?' That sort of thing.

Mind you, Helena used to suffer from exactly the same problem; girls asking her how she managed to have such a good relationship with me and yet still have so many friends. We used to laugh about it. I'd call her Aunt Ag, you know, like Agony; she'd call me Doc, like doctor. I suppose that's rather ironic now.

I was never really jealous of her, never anxious about her ditching me, even though I knew she was a very special sort of person, the sort of person who would attract friends, especially boyfriends, easily.

When she took nine months out, working for this charity in South America, I missed her of course, but I settled down into a comfortable routine. I worked hard and enjoyed it. Regularly, there would be a long white envelope with a South American postmark waiting for me on the doormat. She would tell me about the children – she was working in a school. Yes, she wrote to me excitedly about the plans she had for a trip into the rain forest before she came home.

One August evening, when my mother and father were out, the phone rang. I answered it. Although I knew Helena was due home, deep down I had a nagging worry that she might decide to stay in South America for good. Anyhow, my whole spine tingled with excitement when I heard her voice.

'Hi Doc, it's your old Aunt Ag here. I've got a problem. I've just got back from South America. I'm dying to be taken out for a decent meal, but no-one will invite me.'

Twenty minutes later we were in Casa John's.

The South American sun had given her a deep tan which made her even more beautiful.

'Oh Doc,' she sighed, 'it was great out there, really great, but if you knew the nights I've lain awake simply aching for—'

'For me?' I suggested with a grin.

'No,' she laughed. 'For a slice of Casa John's *Quattro Formaggio*!' She plucked a strand of dripping mozzarella from my chin and wound it round her finger.

She told me all about her work at the school. She showed me pictures of the family she had lived with. And yes, she told me, even more excitedly about her 'jungle stomp', as she insisted on calling it, into the rain forest. She even boasted about the privations she had suffered.

'Bugs, creepy crawlies? You've never seen so many. Not that they bothered *me*.'

We laughed and we chatted all evening. It was only then that I realized just how much I had missed her.

I did notice the nasty red blotch on her cheek. When I saw her again at the weekend, the blotch was still there. Indeed, I thought it seemed larger, redder, more puffy. I noticed too, that she kept touching it.

She saw that I noticed. 'It's the sun. It's not that hot up in the mountains, but the air is thin. It can give you nasty sunburn. The doctor's given me some cream for it. It'll soon clear up.'

She usually spoke with such self-confidence and the lack of conviction in her words was unsettling.

The following Wednesday, we were due to meet some of the others from the Drama Club at Harry's Wine Bar in the High Street. When I called for her she was wearing a head scarf round her face – in August! She looked ridiculous, like she was the Queen or something. Even hidden by the scarf though, it was obvious that her face was swelling.

'What do you keep staring at me like that for?' she snapped.

We only got as far as the end of her road.

'I don't want to meet the others,' she simply said.

'But why not Helly, you've been dying to tell them all about the seven wonders of South America.'

'I just don't want to, that's all. All right?'

Already she was striding back to her house.

'Helly . . .' I grabbed her arm. She pulled away. She wouldn't look at me. She just put her key in the front door.

'Can I come in?' I was conscious that there was a sense of pleading in my voice.

'If you like.'

We sat for the rest of the evening in separate armchairs, watching *Coronation Street* and *Midweek Lottery*. It was dreadful. Her parents poked their grinning heads round the door from time to time, before returning to the garden.

When I came to leave, she wouldn't let me kiss her goodbye. Not even on the cheek. Especially not on the cheek.

'I'll see you tomorrow,' I said.

She shrugged and closed the door.

The next day, I thought about ringing and cancelling, I really did. Perhaps it would have been better if I had. Certainly for me it would have been.

I met her parents on their way out.

'Go on in and wait, Tom, Helena's upstairs,' her mother told me.

'How is she?' I asked.

'She's going back to the doctor's tomorrow to get some more cream,' her mother said.

I closed the door behind and called out, 'Helly, it's me!'

I sat down in the kitchen and starting leafing through a women's magazine.

The house was eerily quiet. I didn't like it. Then, all of a sudden, a horrific scream filled the whole house.

I tore upstairs.

I found her in the bathroom. Her eyes were wild and she was screaming still, clawing at her cheek like some wild animal. I could see where she had scratched her cheek and torn the skin. I could how the cheek had collapsed. I could see the creamy pus oozing from the broken skin. I could see the tiny red spiders crawling out from the scratch and scurrying madly all over her face.

Fighting my nausea, I tried to put my arms around her, but she kicked out and screamed at me in a frenzy.

I couldn't do anything.

I couldn't.

I stumbled down the stairs. Grabbed the phone. Her screaming went on and on. I dialled 999. Misdialled. Dialled again. Still the screaming.

The ambulance came and took her away.

Then I was sick.

I saw Helena once more. When I went to the hospital. The doctor told me it would be unwise for me to see her. But I knew better than him. I *knew* Helena, after all. She had been in the same class as me right from Year Seven.

I had to sign a form. Two nurses accompanied me. There were two locks on the door.

There was no furniture in the room. For her own safety's sake, one of the nurses said, though I didn't quite understand what she meant at the time. The windows were high up, out of reach.

She was sitting in the corner, rocking gently, sort of humming to herself.

'Hi, Auntie Ag,' I said.

She jerked her head up. I saw the scar on her cheek. But it was her eyes that drew my look. They stared uncomprehending, unblinking at me. Then all of a sudden, she was on her feet in no time. She lunged at me. Her fists grabbed at the flesh of my cheeks. Her voice screamed in my ears.

The nurses pulled her off and bundled me out of the room. The doctor shrugged as if to say, 'I told you so.' The wound on Helena's cheek was already healing, he said. After all, the spiders that had hatched under her skin weren't poisonous. But as to Helena's wounded mind . . . that would never heal.

Sometimes when I am taking our dog out for a walk on a Sunday afternoon, I pass Helena's house and see Helena's parents shuffling into their old Metro. They visit her every week.

I've never been out with anybody else. Not after Helena.

DOG'S DINNER

She was just *so* embarrassing!

Lucy watched her mother sitting there on the patio, her feet spread out at right angles on top of the drinks' trolley, her skirt hitched halfway up her thighs, giggling in that *excruciating* schoolgirly voice of hers. She was making love to her mobile phone.

'Oliver, darling! It would be absolutely super if you could make it. Yes . . . it'll only be a small dinner party, just one or two close friends, yourself, of course, included . . . !' She paused for an extra ingratiating giggle. 'What's the word I'm looking for . . . ?'

Pathetic? Lucy thought.

'Intimate.'

Huh! Pukey-pukey! thought Lucy, who is she trying to kid? Actually Lucy knew exactly who it was her mother was trying to kid: Oliver Hutchings, that was who. Oliver Hutchings was only *twenty-three*! Lucy knew this for a fact, because Oliver Hutchings was also *Mr* Hutchings – her English teacher.

'Who *is* Mr Hutchings with? She looks old enough to be his mother!' Lucy had overheard a sixth-former asking a friend on the way out of school one afternoon.

'She is,' Lucy had muttered under her breath. 'At least she's old enough to be *my* mother.'

Lucy had turned quickly on her heel and walked out of school the back way, by the kitchens, so as to avoid bumping into her mother and Mr Hutchings.

And now here was her mother organizing one of her *intimate* dinner parties, for *his* benefit. Lucy knew for certain who the other guests would be: her mother's bosom friends Gushing Giselle and Prattling Pia and their husbands Rory and Martin. Indeed, Lucy over-heard her ringing them up as soon as 'Oliver darling' had been 'booked'. Both Giselle and Pia said, 'Sarah darling, we wouldn't miss it for the world!' Miss the chance of Sarah Gardiner parading her toy boy for all to see? You bet they wouldn't, thought Lucy.

'I suppose I've got to sit there like a dutiful daughter and pass round the peppermint dressing or whatever?' asked Lucy, when her mother told her of her plans.

'You most certainly have not!' A flicker of terror flashed across Mrs Gardiner's eyes. 'I don't want you within a million miles of the dining room.'

'What am I supposed to do, then?' Lucy muttered, pouting.

'I'll get a video in for you to watch in your room.'

She's trying just a little too hard, thought Lucy. 'Make sure it's an eighteen-rated horror one, then,' she replied, just to make her point.

The video was an *X Files* one. Mrs Gardiner was certainly trying hard, very hard indeed.

Lucy heard the front-door bell ring.

Immediately, her mother's friend Pia's excited voice filled the hall. 'Sarah, *darling*, tell me all – and spare no details!' She clucked and cooed like an old hen.

Mrs Gardiner's other friends, Giselle and Rory, arrived next.

'Sarah, your dinner parties are always *so* exciting—' insisted Giselle.

'Unforgettable,' added Rory.

Lucy heard all this and practised throwing-up faces in the mirror.

By the time Mr Hutchings rang the bell, the jury was ready and waiting.

Lucy laid down on her bed and watched the video. It was damaged. There were funny squiggly lines running across it. So she watched a gardening programme on BBC2 instead. This gave a whole new meaning to the words excruciatingly boring.

Lucy dozed off. She awoke to the sound of brakes screeching. She could also hear Giselle's screeching laughter from the dining room below. Her bedside clock said half past nine. She tiptoed down to the kitchen to fix herself a sandwich. The remains of a side of best roast beef sat in the middle of the butcher's table. Not that it tempted Lucy. She was an ardent vegetarian and always had been, ever since the beginning of term.

Lucy felt the warm breeze blowing in from the back door, which was open. She heard a scuffling sound and saw Buster, the family's pet Yorkie, on the doorstep. He had his head in his food bowl. He had been banned from the dinner party too, but at least Mrs Gardiner had had the decency to pass him a few scraps of roast beef for his dinner. He looked up at Lucy – and straight away she knew that something was terribly wrong. Before she had time to take stock, Buster whined, then toppled over, retching and convulsing like mad.

It only took Lucy a second to race round to him, but there was nothing she could do. She stroked his back as he writhed and spewed, then his head suddenly lolled over.

'Mum! Buster's dead!'

As a dinner party-conversation-stopper that line, uttered by a sobbing girl bursting through the dividing doors, does actually take some beating.

The assembled guests froze as one. Rory sat there, his mouth stuffed full of fruit compote, seemingly unable to swallow. Giselle dribbled coffee down her chin, Martin's umpteenth glass of Courvoisier was having trouble making contact with his mouth, while Mr Hutchings's hand had got itself glued to Lucy's mum's knee.

Mrs Gardiner stared at her daughter. Her look said, Go away. I don't want to know about it. Then, without a word, she got up. Mr Hutchings's hand unglued itself from her knee as if by magic. 'I'll come with you,' he purred.

Mrs Gardiner crouched down and stroked Buster behind the ears.

'What happened, Lucy?'

Lucy shrugged. 'He was eating his supper, then he staggered and was sick. Then he just fell over.' She sniffed and swallowed hard. 'I think he's been poisoned,' she found herself saying.

Mrs Gardiner looked at his food bowl. There was still a bit of roast beef left. 'You mean . . . by the meat?'

'That was what he was eating when he . . . when he . . .' Lucy managed not to utter the dreaded 'd' word.

Mrs Gardiner was swaying about rather dizzily. 'But . . . but it came from Hammond's!'

'It came from a cow,' Lucy murmured.

She glowered at her daughter. 'Saints preserve us, you're such a sanctimonious little prig!' she hissed. She turned, staggered across the kitchen and slumped into a chair.

'Sarah?' Mr Hutchings was wide-eyed with worry.

'I think I feel sick.'

Mr Hutchings looked at Lucy.

Lucy shrugged. 'Buster ate the meat. Buster was sick. Buster is dead. You ate the meat. Mum feels sick,' she said, trying to state the facts as clearly and as calmly as possible.

Mrs Gardiner got to her feet and lurched towards the sink, her hand in her mouth.

'What are you doing?' Mr Hutchings yelled at her.

'Trying to make myself sick!'

Lucy took the phone from the wall.

'What are *you* doing?' Mr Hutchings yelled at her.

'Calling an ambulance,' she replied, calmly.

They tumbled into the back of the ambulance like calves boarding a cattle-truck. Mrs Gardiner insisted on being carried, which didn't please the paramedics greatly. Lucy tried to keep words like e-coli, bovine spongiform encephalopathy and listeria out of the conversation, she really did. Not that any of them felt like talking.

They were all whisked through Accident and Emergency like Club Class passengers at an airport. Lucy tagged along behind, for all the world like a stewardess.

'Lucy, don't let them give me a general anaesthetic,' pleaded her mother.

'They won't, Mummy.'

'They do . . . in these places. I've heard about. They'll take something out . . . a length of intestine or a kidney or something without you knowing. Then they sell them to Turkey and places!'

'Mummy. It'll be all right!'

Of course, it was most definitely *not* all right. Not for any of them.

Lucy watched as the long rubber tubes were pushed down her mother's and her dinner-party guests' throats and into their gullets. She listened as the room was filled with the sound of sobbing and retching. For an impressionable girl like Lucy it was a horrific experience, though for Sarah, Martin, Pia, Giselle, Rory and Oliver, it was far worse.

Lucy's mum rather wished that they *had* given her a general anaesthetic.

Mr Hutchings collected his car the next day. He just sneaked up the drive and drove off. Lucy's mum tried ringing him all morning, but it seemed he had taken the phone off the hook. Buster was buried in the pets' graveyard by the rhubarb patch, where he joined three rabbits, two hamsters and a white rat.

And that might have been that. But then, just before tea time, there was a ring at the front door. Lucy went. A balding man in glasses stood there, nervously shuffling from one foot to the other.

'Ah . . . could I speak to your father?'

She shook her head.

'It's er . . . quite important.' The man wriggled and twisted like an expiring worm.

'He's not here.'

'When will he be back?'

'December. His next leave. He works in Riyadh.'

'Can I help you?' Mrs Gardiner appeared. She was still pale and drawn from her experience on the wrong end of the stomach pump, but she managed to put on one of her ear-to-ear smiles.

She took the visitor through to the drawing room.

'I'm so sorry about your dog,' he blurted out.

Mrs Gardiner frowned. 'How do you know about our dog?'

'I'm the driver.'

'I'm sorry . . . ?'

'I was driving the car that ran him over.'

Mrs Gardiner's jaw dropped. Lucy quickly back-tracked out of the room, but she stood in the hall, listening.

'He managed to stagger back here, didn't he?'

Mrs Gardiner said nothing.

'I'm afraid I panicked. I drove straight off. But I couldn't sleep a wink last night. I felt I had to do the proper thing and come and tell you. Even though there's nothing I can do. I hope he didn't suffer too much. I'm sorry.'

'Excuse me,' said Mrs Gardiner. Before Lucy knew it, her mother had dashed past her and had hurtled into the cloakroom.

The hit-and-run driver saw Lucy peering round the door. 'He didn't suffer, did he?' he asked in a tone of grovelling desperation.

'No, no,' she smiled, sweetly. '*Buster* didn't suffer at all.'

THE HANDS
OF
OLD
MISS SUMMERS

SOMERS
FRESH

HAMPTON TIMES

OMAN, 72,
HORROR
ATTACK

FIVE
TOMATO
KETCHUP

THE HANDS OF OLD MISS SUMMERS

Susan Bulstrode was the first person in the Sixth Form to pass her test. Mr and Mrs Bulstrode had no qualms about their daughter borrowing the family car.

'We don't use the car that often, particularly at evenings and weekends,' her father had said, 'unless I'm taking your mother out for a spin the country.' Both he and his wife were in their late fifties.

Susan was a sensible sort of girl, after all. She was a helpful sort of girl, too. She borrowed the car so that she could help Brown Owl take some of the Brownies on a trip to a local children's farm. She was, of course, more than happy for the vicar to put her down on the rota as a volunteer driver, willing to collect and return the odd housebound old lady to and from matins. Every Friday evening she drove her mother to Somersbury's super-market out at the new retail park to do the weekly shopping, so that her father could spend more time tending his koi carp.

But this Friday evening, Susan was shopping alone. Her mother had one of her headaches, for which she blamed the weather. 'All this sunshine! In March! It's unnatural.'

Susan's father was willing to go with her, but she could tell he was itching to get out to his carp. In any case, her mother was petrified of being left at home alone.

'Supposing the phone goes?' That was her great fear. 'Mrs Murdle told me a terrible story about a friend of her sister's who had nuisance calls. You'll never guess where they traced the caller to—'

'That was in Scotland,' interrupted Susan's father, who clearly believed that the country north of Berwick was populated by hairy club-wielding savages.

'It's all right. I *can* manage to pick up a bit of shopping on my own.' Susan chuckled to herself at her parents' fluster.

So, this Friday evening, Susan Bulstrode was alone.

Shopping didn't take her long. Without her mother fussing about whether two pounds of succulent Special Offer Frozen Garden Peas were better value than one kilo of juicy Lo-Price Frozen Petits Pois, she got from aisle one (onions) to aisle fifteen (deodorants) in no time at all. And this despite the usual hordes of Friday night shoppers.

It was as she was loading the flimsy plastic bags into the boot that she first noticed the old lady sitting on one of the hard red metal seats at the bus stop.

She reminded Susan of the old ladies she ferried to and from matins. She wore a shapeless apple-green raincoat, the sort you could buy for a few pounds from any charity shop, stout brown lace-up shoes, a grey hat trimmed with fake fur and, despite the unseasonable warmth of the evening, a woollen scarf around her neck. She look worried and forlorn. Susan went across to her.

'Are you waiting for the bus?'

The old lady nodded. She looked nervously away.

Susan looked down the timetable. 'There aren't any more buses tonight,' she said, calmly, so as not to alarm the old lady. 'The last one left at six. They cancelled the evening ones, I seem to remember, because of all the vandalism.'

116

The old lady clasped her one carrier bag of shopping even more closely to her chest. 'Oh dear,' she muttered. 'What shall I do, then?'

Susan understood her concern. She had seen the headline in the local evening paper: WOMAN, 72, IN HORROR AXE ATTACK.

Susan, of course, was a helpful kind of girl. 'I can give you a lift back into town, if you like.'

'No, no, my dear, I couldn't possibly . . .' The old lady fidgeted anxiously. 'I can get a taxi.'

'At the prices they charge? Don't be silly,' scolded Susan, sounding ever-so grown-up. And before she could argue any further, the old lady found herself being steered firmly, but gently, towards Susan's parents' car.

'I know what the police say,' said Susan, with a quick laugh, 'about taking lifts from strangers, but I can assure you, I'm not Jack the Ripper!'

The old lady smiled hesitantly.

'See,' laughed Susan, pointing at a badge on the back windscreen, 'Guides! That's me. My name is Susan by the way. Susan Bulstrode.'

The old lady seemed to relax a little. Susan took out the patchwork cushion she always used for her matins trips, plumped it up and placed it on the passenger seat for the old lady. Then guiding the old lady's arm, she helped her in. Her stockings were woolly and thick – thicker even than her mother's, Susan realized.

Susan fixed the seat-belt round the old lady and belted it up. Then she carefully worked her way out of the complicated one-way system and out onto the bypass.

'Where do you live?' asked Susan.

The old lady mumbled nervously. Susan knew just what the trouble was. 'Where do you live?' she asked again, raising her voice by thirty decibels. Most of the old ladies she took to and from matins were hard-of-hearing.

'Er . . . London Road.' The old lady spoke in a voice barely above a whisper.

Susan smiled brightly. 'In the old people's flats at the back of the undertakers?'

The old lady returned Susan's smile briefly and nodded. 'Yes, yes!'

'I know the flats well,' said Susan. 'I often pick up Mrs Pennyfather and take her to St Stephen's.'

'Oh, that's er . . . nice,' said the old lady.

'You're not a churchgoer?' asked Susan.

'No . . . no dear,' said the old lady. 'I'm er . . . chapel.'

They were speeding along the bypass towards the main road into town. The sun dropped quickly behind the downs, as it always did at this time of year. Susan switched the headlights on. Traffic sped past her in the outside lanes, lighting up the interior of her car in a succession of bright, white flashes.

'I'm sorry,' said Susan. 'I never asked you your name.'

'Er . . . Miss . . . Miss Summers.'

'Miss Summers did you say?'

'That's right, my dear.'

Susan frowned. Odd, she thought. Mrs Pennyfather gossiped like mad about all her neighbours, but Susan was sure she had never mentioned a Miss Summers.

'It's nice and friendly there, isn't it?' said Susan to Miss Summers.

Miss Summers nodded.

'Do you know Mrs Pennyfather?'

'Er . . . not really,' mumbled Miss Summers. 'You see, I only moved in last week.'

Susan swallowed hard. She was sure Mrs Pennyfather would have mentioned if someone had moved in. After all, for someone to move, someone else would have had to move out – and that meant somebody *dying*.

Mrs Pennyfather would have been bound to mention someone 'passing on' as she called it.

Susan felt her hands tighten on the steering-wheel. 'Which number are you?' she asked, unable to stem a slight quiver in her voice.

'Umm . . .' Miss Summers was thinking hard. 'Number two.'

Number two was Mrs Pennyfather's flat! No, no, Susan thought to herself, don't be silly, Susan Bulstrode. There's a perfectly rational explanation. Miss Summers is just a bit doolally. Yes, that's it. Old ladies often forget their names and where they live. Poor old soul, thought Susan.

Miss Summers. Susan turned the name over in her head. She was sure Mrs Pennyfather hadn't talked of a Miss Summers, but somehow the name had a familiar ring to it.

They approached the flyover and the turn-off for the town. The harsh glow of rows of sodium street lights filled the car. Susan signalled left, changed down and briefly looked down at the gear-stick as she did so. She noticed Miss Summers's carrier bag. *Somersbury's For Finer Foods* it said.

Somersbury . . . Summers . . . Stop it, you're

getting as panicky as your mother, Susan Bulstrode.

It was at that moment Susan caught sight of Miss Summers's hands. They were large and dark. Thick black hairs ran along all the way down her fingers. Susan's head began to pound in panic. She was sure. Miss Summers's hands were not the hands of an old lady. They were not the hands of any kind of lady. They were a man's hands.

'Oh yes, Susan, we're all very friendly in the flats,' Miss Summers was saying. 'Why my dear, whatever is the matter—'

His sudden look of sheer malice told Susan that he knew that she knew the truth. Susan also knew she had to be out of the car as soon as possible. With her left elbow she surreptitiously pushed her seat-belt release. Then she slammed on the brakes. It had only been a few months ago that she had taken her test; she knew all about emergency stops.

The man who was Miss Summers shot forward in surprise, then swore as he found his seat-belt locked round him. Susan opened her door and pulled at the ignition keys. She had to pull at them twice; she felt a man's hairy hand reaching out for her arm.

'Come back, you stupid fool!' rasped a deep, masculine voice.

Susan's loud, manic scream scared even herself. It shocked her attacker too and in the brief moment that she had him off guard, she wrenched herself away. And ran. Across the slip road. Over the flyover. She was aware of cars hooting her, but none of them stopped. She didn't expect them to. She didn't *want* any of them to stop, for fear that one of them might somehow be *him*.

On and on she ran, losing breath all the time, feeling the stabbing of a stitch in her side growing sharper by the second. The houses got smaller, the street lights got closer. She wasn't seeing where she was going. Something hit her. She felt she was swimming in a dark, dark sea. No, she wasn't swimming, she was drowning. She heard a thud. Then it all went black.

The young male nurse explained what had happened. 'You ran into a jogger – literally. He saw what a state you were in, took you into the nearest house and dialled the ambulance.'

Later, after her mother and father had gone back home, a police officer came in and sat down by her hospital bedside.

'We found your car, Susan.'

'Did you find . . . the man?'

The police officer shook his head. 'But we did find his shopping bag.' He raised his eyebrows. 'You've been very lucky, Susan.'

'What do you mean?'

'Inside the shopping bag we found . . . not the usual Somersbury's fare.'

'No . . . ?'

'Inside the shopping bag we found a blood-stained hatchet.'

WHAT SHALL WE DO WITH

GRANNY SiMPKiNS?

WHAT
SHALL WE DO WiTH
GRANNY SiMPKiNS?

They were a typical family on holiday, the Smalls.

Mr Small, in shorts, led the way. He was reading from a hefty guide-book. Next came Mrs Small, most of her face covered by a pair of large plastic-framed sunglasses. Their teenage children, Matthew and Rebecca, mooched behind. Finally, clutching the strap of an enormous handbag came Mrs Small's mother, Granny Simpkins.

'This is the place!' called Mr Small, excitedly. He gave the guide-book a final glance before stuffing it into the pockets of his shorts. '"Delightful café, offering simple, local cooking served in a delightful ambience."'

'What's ambience?' Rebecca asked her brother.

'Dunno. Some sort of sauce?' suggested Matthew.

'I hate sauce,' said Rebecca.

'That's more like it!' Matthew nodded to a large sign in the window: BURGER & CHIPS!!!

They followed their parents into the café. There was a large, vacant table in the corner, by the window.

'Come on, mother-in-law!' Mr Small called. But old Mrs Simpkins stood rooted to a spot just inside the door. Her head was cocked slightly to one side, as if she was listening intently.

'I'm not eating in here!'

'Mother . . .' Mrs Small's eyes were already darting this way and that with embarrassment.

Rebecca and Matthew groaned.

'Why not?' Mr Small asked his mother-in-law in a placatory voice.

Old Mrs Simpkins glanced about her, furtively. 'It's full of foreigners!' she hissed.

'Of course it's full of foreigners!' shouted her son-in-law, much louder than he had planned.

Every diner in the café had stopped eating and was looking at the Smalls.

Mr Small lowered his voice. 'It's full of foreigners because we happen to be abroad! This is,' he added, enunciating his words with deliberate slowness, 'the south of France!'

Old Mrs Simpkins didn't hear him. She had

already marched out of the café.

Mrs Small went out to remonstrate with her mother. Mr Small went out to be with his wife. Matthew and Rebecca sighed and left the 'delightful café, offering simple, local cooking served in a delightful ambience' – and with it any hope of burger and chips.

'She's always doing it!' moaned Rebecca. 'Spoiling it!'

Rebecca had never been more right in her life. Granny Simpkins had been the curse of their summer holiday. To be honest, they would have preferred it if she had not come with them at all.

'She's too old to sleep in a tent!' Matthew had protested.

'She won't sleep in a tent. She'll sleep in the camper van,' their father had explained.

Rebecca had groaned.

'It's *her* camper van, after all,' Mrs Small had reasoned.

This was true. When Grandad Simpkins had been alive, he and Granny Simpkins had spent every summer travelling in their camper van. Only in the British Isles, of course; never abroad.

'It wouldn't be fair to leave her on her own

in the granny flat,' Mrs Small had argued. 'She's not been very well of late, not since that last heart attack.'

What all the Smalls knew, of course, was that they would be the sole beneficiaries of Granny Simpkins's will. Mr Small had set his heart on a four-wheeled-drive jeep, Mrs Small pined for a conservatory, Matthew knew exactly what sort of computer he wanted and Rebecca absolutely *needed* a whole new wardrobe of designer clothes. They couldn't afford to antagonise Granny Simpkins into changing her mind.

Nevertheless, Matthew and Rebecca had huffed and puffed and protested.

'Once we get on to a decent site, Granny will be quite happy to snooze all day in the camper van reading back copies of the *People's Friend*,' Mrs Small had said.

'Reading what?' Rebecca had asked.

'You know, that old biddy's magazine full of stories about nerds in kilts falling in lurve on mountain-tops with soppy-looking birds in cardigans,' Matthew had explained for his sister's benefit.

'You seem to be very familiar with it . . .'

Matthew had made a face at his sister.

'The point is,' Mrs Small had continued, 'you two will be quite free to go off and do your own thing.'

But that was where she had been wrong.

At the first campsite, while she had been supposedly snoozing with a hundred and twenty back copies of the *People's Friend*, Granny Simpkins had actually been following Matthew and Rebecca – making sure they didn't get into trouble. Which was how she had come to find them lounging about the campsite bar drinking beer.

At the second site, a smart four-star place with a huge swimming pool, Granny Simpkins had objected to the number of topless sunbathers, which she had seen as a corrupting influence on Matthew and, it has to be said, his dad. They'd moved on, at the crack of dawn, after only one night.

'Why we couldn't have stayed in England, I don't know,' Granny Simpkins had muttered.

On their first evening at the third site, while Matthew and Rebecca had been enjoying the camp disco with some French teenagers they had met, they had been horrified to see their grandmother storm in, march up to the stage, tell the DJ she couldn't sleep for all the racket he was making and pull the plugs from their sockets. The Smalls were asked to leave first thing the following morning.

And now had come the incident at the café . . .

They walked back to the campsite in silence; a heavy, brooding silence. They'd got back to their pitch before anyone said anything. And then, of course, it was Granny Simpkins who spoke.

'A nice cup of tea and a couple of digestive biscuits will do me,' she announced, making for the motor caravan. 'And then, as my company seem surplus to requirements, I'll turn in.'

'Turn into what?' muttered Rebecca under her breath, but loud enough for her brother to hear.

'Good night!' Granny Simpkins stepped into the motor caravan and closed the door behind her.

Rebecca and Matthew stood there, kicking at the dusty ground with their trainers. Mrs Small looked at her husband. 'What are *we* going to eat?'

'Don't look at me like that, she's your mother!' snapped Mr Small.

'But we still can't eat her,' muttered Rebecca.

'Don't try and be funny, Rebecca!'

'We can't go into the motor caravan to cook, if she's gone to bed,' sighed Matthew.

The French family from the adjoining pitch walked past, their chunky sweaters draped round their shoulders. They were obviously going off into the village to eat. They called out a hearty *'Bonsoir!'* to the Smalls. They received glum looks back.

'There's some bread and camembert left over from lunch,' ventured Mrs Small, 'but it's in the caravan.'

The groans were audible.

'We could go back to the café,' said Rebecca, quietly.

The others did not reply.

'She'll be asleep,' added Rebecca.

'Supposing she wakes up?' asked Mrs Small.

'She won't,' said Rebecca. 'The first couple of hours of sleep are the soundest.' She was taking GCSE Biology, and so, of course, was an absolute expert on anything related to Human Behaviour.

Various aromas of barbecuing steak, grilling onions and sizzling garlic drifted across the campsite, teasing the Smalls' nostrils.

Mr Small looked at his watch. 'I reckon she'll be off in about fifteen minutes.'

Matthew nodded. 'Nobody can read a *People's Friend* story and stay awake for much longer than that.'

'We'll check her in fifteen,' said Mr Small.

In fact, it was just twelve minutes later when they approached the motor caravan; their hunger was getting the better of them. Granny Simpkins had left the key in the rear door, so Mr Small unlocked the driver's door. They listened hard, heard nothing. They clambered over the driver's seat and peered into the back.

She was tucked up in the narrow divan bed, next to the dining table. She didn't stir. Not even when Matthew whispered, 'Night, Granny!'

Mr Small locked the van. 'She'll be safe enough in there,' he said with an uneasy frown. 'You don't get intruders about this early.'

Mrs Small shuddered at the thought; though in truth, she was more scared at what her mother would say if she ever discovered that her daughter and her family had gone off and left her alone in a motor caravan on a French camping site packed full of *foreigners*. Then she turned, and taking her husband's

133

arm, followed her children out through the still bustling campsite and back up the hill into the village.

Once they'd had a couple of glasses of the very palatable local wine, Mr and Mrs Small's worries about Granny Simpkins soon vanished. Once they'd had a couple more glasses of wine, Mr and Mrs Small didn't notice Rebecca and Matthew helping themselves to the bottle, as well.

In short, the Smalls, *sans* Granny Simpkins, had a great time and a great meal. Rebecca and Matthew's burgers were succulent and their chips plentiful. Mr & Mrs Small's *piments farcis* (stuffed peppers) were . . . well, everything you would expect stuffed peppers to be.

'One of the best meals I've ever had,' declared Mr Small, belching loudly.

They wandered giddily back to the campsite in the moonlight.

They passed Lorenzo, the tall, good-looking Italian boy from the camp shop, and he smiled at Rebecca. She was already wondering what she might need to go to the shop to buy in the morning.

A group of boys was returning from the shores of the nearby lake, where they'd been playing volleyball. Matthew thought he might join them tomorrow.

Their light-heartededness soon dissipated as they approached Granny Simpkins' motor caravan. They were all a little nervous.

'Supposing something's happened?' Matthew blurted out.

'Supposing she's *awake*!' Rebecca whispered.

'Stop the chattering!' hissed Mr Small.

'It's not me who's chattering, it's my teeth,' muttered Rebecca.

'Rebecca. Don't try to be funny,' snorted her mum. She was tense, not in the mood for jokes.

'Shhh! All of you!' Mr Small unlocked the driver's door of the motor caravan.

They crept over the seat.

There was Granny Simpkins. Just as they had left her. She didn't stir, not even when Matthew yelled 'aargh!' as he banged his head on the door-frame. She didn't stir, not even when Rebecca guffawed loudly at the sight of her grandmother lying there with her mouth wide open.

'She's sleeping like a baby,' whispered Mr Small.

But it had been many years since Mr Small had seen a baby sleeping.

The Smalls scrambled out of the motor caravan, all four of them giggling like naughty children.

Rebecca was first to wake next morning. The sun was already high and the inside of her bedroom in the large continental tent was already hot to the touch. She slipped on her T-shirt and shorts. She wanted to get washed quickly, so that she could get up to the shop and buy . . . anything, so long as it meant she could hear Lorenzo's husky Italian voice.

When she got back from the shower block, her family were still asleep. Even Granny Simpkins wasn't up. Rebecca needed to get into the motor caravan. She had to dry her hair before it went all frizzy in the sun, and the motor caravan had an electric socket for the hairdryer.

She tried the rear door. It was still locked. She tried calling her grandmother. There was no answer. She peered into the windows. The curtains were still drawn. She felt her stomach tying itself into a knot. She ran into the tent.

'Dad! Mum! Granny's not up!'

Mr Small turned over. 'Let her sleep then . . .'

Mrs Small briefly opened her eyes. Saw

the day, then quickly shut them.

'But Dad . . .' Rebecca wanted to say how late it was; how hot the motor caravan was; how it must be like an oven inside. Instead, she saw the keys lying on her dad's shorts at the foot of his camp-bed and grabbed them.

Matthew had heard the commotion and was up too.

They unlocked the motor caravan and clambered in. The air was hot enough to poach eggs in. There was a strange, sickly smell, that might have been camembert cheese . . .

Granny Simpkins was still tucked up in the narrow divan bed, next to the dining table. She didn't stir. Not even when Matthew whispered, 'Granny?' Not even when Matthew yelled at the top of his voice, 'Granny!'

The night before Rebecca had laughed at the sight of her grandmother lying there with her mouth wide open. Now she screamed.

Still the old lady didn't stir.

There was no doubt about it. Granny Simpkins was dead.

'Open the windows!' Mr Small spoke in a strange kind of half-shout, half-whisper; half-shout because he was in a panic, half-whisper because even though he was panicked some-thing was telling him not to arouse the attention of his fellow campers.

'No! Don't open the windows!' If anything was going to arouse the attention of the campers, it was going to be the smell . . . 'Yes . . . ! Open them!' Not opening the windows on a summer's morning with the temperature soaring would surely invite inquisitive looks, too.

Matthew found his sister huddled up and shaking in her sleeping-bag. She had squirmed her way out of the motor caravan as soon as Mr Small had rushed over to see what all the screaming was about.

'You OK?'

Rebecca nodded and stifled a sniff; although it was not, it had to be said, a particularly tearful one.

'What are they going to do?' she asked.

Matthew shrugged. 'Dad's pulled the sheet up over her face.'

Rebecca nodded again. Yes, yes, that was what you did, of course. She remembered seeing it in films. 'They'll have to tell someone . . . the authorities.' They did that in films too.

Matthew sighed.

*   *   *

The Smalls sat in their folding chairs under the brightly striped awning. A pot of coffee stood in the middle of the picnic table, untouched. No more than four metres in front of them was the motor caravan, its windows open, its doors locked. None of them could take their eyes off it.

'You've got to tell someone . . . the authorities,' suggested Rebecca. Mrs Small nodded.

'Who do we tell?' asked Mr Small.

'The police?' suggested Matthew.

'Have you seen any police in this place? That little fat git with the beer gut and pill-box hat who sits about in the café smoking Gauloises all day? He's only a souped-up traffic warden.'

'Perhaps we'd better drive to Avignon, then.' This was Mrs Small's suggestion.

'What, with Granny still in bed?' Matthew's jaw dropped.

Rebecca's mind was on something else. 'Do you think she died when we were out, last night?'

No-one looked at her.

'So we tell the police in Avignon that your mother's died. What then?' Mr Small looked his wife straight in the face. His expression was like that of a prosecution lawyer with a weak defendant in the witness box.

Mrs Small shrugged.

'This is France! Have you any idea of the paperwork involved? Have you any idea of what could go wrong? Who else might have to get involved – notaries, lawyers, doctors, town-hall officials, all sorts? And they'll need bribes or tips. Is your French up to it?'

He knew very well that it wasn't. Neither was his, let alone Rebecca's or Matthew's.

'We need the Embassy,' said Mrs Small.

'We're not in Paris.'

'We've got to go and find *someone*,' said Rebecca desperately.

'Wherever we go, we've got to take her,' muttered Matthew.

There was a pause: a pause filled with the sound of excited French voices, as the Smalls' fellow campers busied themselves over their breakfasts.

'Let's take her home,' said Mrs Small.

'To England?'

'Do you think she would've wanted to be left in France? Buried here, even? She hated it!'

'But how . . . ?' Mr Small frowned, hardly daring to contemplate the possibilities.

'On the roof-rack. Rolled up inside the tent.' Mrs Small did not blanch. 'It's not eight yet. We could be at the tunnel by midnight. Back in London before dawn. Then we can call Doc McPherson.' Doc McPherson was a family friend.

'Supposing they stop us at customs?' Mr Small had a great fear of Customs and Excise officers. He watched *The Knock*.

'Nobody stops anyone at Customs any more,' Mrs Small attempted a laugh. 'European Community and all that. And if they did, we aren't doing anything illegal are we? I mean, bringing your own mother home, even if she is dead, well, it's not as if she's a consignment of heroin, is it?'

The Smalls raised their large continental tent high above their heads, struggling to roll it on to the roof-rack of the motor caravan.

'*Bonjour!*' The French family from the adjoining site waved cheerily; their swimming towels slung about their shoulders. Then, to the horror of the Smalls, they ran across, and lifting the tent from their own aching arms, tossed it like a garlic sausage on to the roof of the motor caravan.

'Er . . . thank you, *merci*,' stammered Mr Small.

'*De rien!*' cried the French father, spreading his arms in a dismissive gesture. '*Bon voyage!*'

They drove northwards across France all morning; kilometre after kilometre of straight narrow roads. It was not until the early afternoon that they realized they'd not eaten since the night before. They stopped in a small town where the pavements were littered with brightly-topped tables.

Rebecca and Matthew's burger and chips were not quite as succulent and as plentiful as the previous evening's, but they were good, nevertheless. Mr and Mrs Small's *boeuf bourgignon* was passable.

They hurried along the busy pavements, keen to get back to the car park and on their way.

They stood for some time, staring open-mouthed at the now empty bay where they had left their motor caravan as if they believed that were they all to stare hard enough, the motor caravan – and Granny Simpkins – would reappear.

Then Mrs Small sat down by the waters of a particularly acrid French drain and wept. Mr Small sat down and cursed. Eventually Rebecca said, 'What do we do now?'

'There's only one thing we can do,' said Mr Small. He cashed in his remaining traveller's cheques and they made their way home to London, courtesy of French Railways and Eurostar, without further ado.

Neither the motor caravan, nor Granny Simpkins were ever recovered.

Granny Simpkins's will lies safe in the keeping of an elderly solicitor in Surrey. At the moment, of course, he is completely unaware of her untimely demise. But solicitors are a meticulous and inquisitive breed, so who knows, in time he may get round to asking some very difficult questions indeed.

THE END

AMAZING ADVENTURE STORIES
Collected by Tony Bradman

I almost laughed out loud. Except that the pistol was wavering all over the room. Then suddenly it went off . . .

Ever wondered what you would do if you came face to face with a Nazi parachutist in the Second World War, or were held hostage in the middle of nowhere for your dad's riches? What if you were marooned on a desert island on your way to Australia? Or caught up with a murderess?

Tony Bradman has collected ten action-packed adventure stories from a team of top authors such as Malorie Blackman, Robert Westall, Douglas Hill and Helen Dunmore in this fast-moving and gripping anthology. Your nerves will never be the same again!

'Excitement, fear and suspense in equal measure . . . all the stories are thoroughly entertaining'
School Librarian

0 552 52768 8

CORGI BOOKS